Endorsements

Fa
Stephen Lunn (no relation),

Pacy, entertaining, funny.
Charles Pither, STARC

Fiction firmly rooted in reality.
Colin Tudge, author of The Great Re-Think

Amusing, fast-paced, memorable.
Prof. Riki Therivel

Seriously funny.
Cathy Galvin, founder of the Word Factory

A powerful new voice.
Linda Proud, award-winning novelist

By the same author

FICTION
The Price of Dormice

NON-FICTION
Miss, Does it Matter Which Way Round This Goes?

WE'RE NOT GETTING DIVORCED

and other stories

To Berinsfield Library

Steve Lunn

STEVE LUNN

*We're Not Getting Divorced
and other stories*
Steve Lunn

First published in Great Britain in 2024 by Oxford eBooks Ltd.

Copyright © 2024 Steve Lunn

Cover image based on the painting *Summer Spey Swim*, by Imogen Rigden.

The right of Steve Lunn to be identified as the author of this work has been asserted by them in accordance with the Copyright, Design and Patents Act 1988.

All rights reserved. No part of this publication may be reproduced, transmitted, or stored in a retrieval system, in any form or by any means, without permission in writing from the publisher, nor be otherwise circulated in any form of binding or cover other than that in which it is published and without a similar condition being imposed on the subsequent purchaser. No part of this publication may be read by or used to train an artificial intelligence.

This work is entirely fictitious. The names, characters, organisations, institutions and incidents portrayed in it are either the products of the author's imagination or are used in a fictitious manner, and are not to be construed as real. Any resemblance to actual events or actual persons, living or dead, is entirely co-incidental.

Set Out Running was first published in the Amsterdam Quarterly in the summer 2023 edition, and is reprinted here with permission.

ISBN 978-1-910779-45-3

British Library Cataloguing in Publication Data.

A catalogue record for this book is available from the British Library.

Oxford eBooks

Produced and Typeset by Oxford eBooks Ltd.
www.oxford-ebooks.com

To my wife Imogen Rigden
without whom I wouldn't hear a robin sing
amongst many other things.

CONTENTS

All is Bright	1
Vector Analysis	7
Give and Forgive	11
Set Out Running	17
Why Don't We Find Out?	21
The Tide Turned	31
Party Wall	37
Ridiculous	45
You Could Cut Hair	55
We're Not Getting Divorced	63
A Little Pirouette On The Landing	77
End Notes	83
Acknowledgements	85
About the Author	87
Extract from The Price of Dormice	89

There will come a time when you believe everything is finished. That will be the beginning.

Louis L'Amour

Most endings in our lives contain the seeds of new beginnings, and all beginnings contain the seeds of many possible ends. Busy making other plans and constantly biffed by the vagaries of outrageous fortune, we nurture and crush these seeds willy-nilly in how we live our lives, often below the level of our conscious awareness.

These stories are about endings and beginnings. And about justice and fairness, humility and compassion, love and madness and autonomy. Some may throw light into life's dim and cobwebbed corners, others walk well-trodden paths. Above all they are meant to be entertaining reads. I hope you enjoy them.

Steve Lunn,
Le Diben, Plougasnou,
13th September, 2024

All is Bright

JACK AND I married fifty-six years ago. We were just teenagers. It's only natural I feel lonely without him, but knowing that doesn't help. I spend my days playing his records, reading his books, and trying to stop my mind coming up with things I need to tell him when he gets home. It's two months since he died and I'm in all sorts of trouble.

I'm in the sitting room with the curtains drawn. I've got one of Jack's old LPs on the record player. *Folking Christmas*, it's called. Though the 'ol' of *Folking* is asterisked over, so the title might be open to interpretation. By Adam and Eve Anwick, folk singers and guitar-players. They did this one album then were never heard of again, according to Jack. It's all Christmas songs, played and sung as if they mean something. Which they do, when you think about it.

Jack couldn't resist whistling along with some of them. Always out of tune, to my ears. That's when I'd go and put the kettle on. He'd say he was adding a descant, as if that explained it. This first track on side A, *In the Bleak Mid-Winter*, was a regular whistle-along. He said they'd recorded the songs in railway stations when they were on tour, this one in Widnes. I'm not sure where Widnes is, and I don't know how he knew or where the other tracks were done. You often hear noises in the background that could be trains coming and going and announcements on the PA. But I lose myself in their lovely harmonies, and imagine myself sitting there with a ticket in my pocket, young again, going somewhere, waiting to hear my destination called.

All is Bright

I've got a ticket for my final destination now, in a small bottle in the fridge.

We met in Dublin in 1966, the year this LP came out. I was staying for a week with my Aunt Mary, my mum's sister. I loved it, I felt free as a bird. I could just take a bus into the city and walk round doing anything. Everyone was so kind. One sunny Saturday I was enjoying a really good busker on Grafton Street. A young man standing next to me was whistling along with the tune, and I said, 'Do you know this song? I like it.' As much to stop him whistling as because I wanted to know.

It worked. He looked down at me and said, 'Why aye, I do. Dirty Old Town. It's a love song, ye ken. But to a town, not a woman.'

I loved his accent. 'Where do you come from?' I said.

And he said something that sounded like 'Sunnalun', and I said 'Sunderland?' and he said 'Aye,' and we started chatting and we didn't stop until a few weeks ago. He was eighteen, studying Mech Eng in Newcastle. I was seventeen, training as a secretary. We married the following year, before my first started to show.

Here's the last track on Side A, *Ding Dong Merrily On High*. One Christmas Eve we skipped over Old Elvet Bridge in Durham, breaking our lungs with that almost endless *'Gloria'*, shouting out *'Hosanna in excelsis'* as loud as we could with our last gasps, really loving it. I've no idea what it actually means. Never wondered about it before. Doesn't matter now.

I'll turn the LP over. Sadder songs on side B. *The Coventry Carol*, it starts with, about Herod commanding the slaughter of every boy in Bethlehem aged less than two. What was that like, for their families? And for the little boys of course. Terrible. I've never wondered about that either.

We made a pact, a few years ago. I didn't think we'd ever

actually do it. His treatment first time round had been awful. Mine wasn't much fun either, but it worked, and five years on I'm almost good as new. His knocked him back completely, turned him into an old man. Or an old woman, as he said when his breasts started growing. He got to see his first great-grandchild, and was grateful for that. But if it ever came back, he'd not go through it all again. Surgery, radio, chemo. Hormones and hope. He'd rather die. He made me promise I'd help him, not fight him. And he'd do the same for me, if I wanted, if that was how it worked out.

It hasn't come back for me yet.

It won't, now.

I worked in prisons once, setting up systems in education and rehab, and training the people who were going to run them, mostly prisoners who were trusted to behave themselves, usually lifers. Not many wanted to talk about what they'd done, but two did. They'd both killed their wives. They both said the same thing, in so many words. *She was terrified of dying in pain, like her mum had, or her sister. When the pain got really bad, she begged me. I had no choice.* I remember thinking *they would say something like that, wouldn't they?* I didn't pay much attention at the time, my concern was getting them trained. I wish I'd listened better, tried to understand.

What happened to those two would have been just like what's happening to me now. Your life partner has just died. You're in pieces. You were only doing what your old love wanted, trying to do the kind thing. The right thing. So you tell the truth.

My lawyer's quite nice. Very young. She says the inquest will return a verdict of unlawful killing, then I'll be in the system and charged. She's advising me to plead guilty. As far as the law goes I am guilty, she says, so I don't have much choice. I suppose she knows.

'It'll mean a lighter sentence, and you'll be able to work in the prison library,' she says, as if I should be pleased. 'At least you won't need training. And with good behaviour you'll be out quite soon, six or seven years at most.'

In seven years I'll be eighty-two. How long would I have left? What kind of life would I have? I loved him, and kept faith with him. But our kids don't know what happened, and they're bound to find out. What will they say? And their kids? And how will they treat me in seven years' time, when I'm a time-served killer? They'll not want to know. No-one will. I'll be completely alone.

Jack was in pain, the drugs weren't touching it. He was an engineer, he always wanted to be in control. We researched it together. He decided on hemlock. I gathered it from a river in Cornwall where he used to fish when we were on holiday. Sometimes on summer evenings we'd sit quiet and still into the darkest time, just watching, hoping to see an otter. And we did. And all sorts of other things.

I boiled up the hemlock roots, made a sort of herbal tea. He drank it down. 'It's not bad,' he said. 'Tastes like tonic.' Those were his last words, actually. It was like taking the dog to the vet. One moment he's looking you in the eye, slightly wary but not really frightened or in pain. Then the life in his eyes just goes out. It only takes a couple of seconds.

He drank less than half of what I'd made. I put the rest in a little bottle. It's kept fine in the fridge for a few weeks, while I put my affairs in order. I've got it set up now, with ice and a slice and a drop of gin.

I'm waiting for the last track on Side B, *Silent Night*. There's a station announcer in the background. You can hardly hear her to begin with. They sing the first verse twice through in harmony. In the background the announcer gets slowly louder: '... calling at Birmingham, Manchester,

Lancaster, Carlisle. Glasgow, Stirling, Inverness.' There's an instrumental, then more singing that you can hardly hear because by then the announcer drowns out everything else. I don't like it, it spoils the music. I can't understand why they didn't wait and record it again, when the Inverness train had left. With any luck I'll not hear that bit.

Here we are, the last track's starting.

I drink it down.

It doesn't taste much like tonic to me.

I close my eyes, listen.

They had such lovely voices.

Silent night, holy night
All is calm, all is bright

Vector Analysis

BANX AND FLATFACE run from the elevator, across the platform, through doors emitting pre-close beeps. A robot says 'Please stand clear of the closing doors'. Banx reaches up with his left and grabs a grab-bar. The doors hiss shut, everyone breathes. The train lurches.

Packed Victoria Line passengers bend to the Gs of acceleration crossed with side to side wobble and random buck. Crap shockers, Banx thinks. Or crap track-laying. Or both.

He sniffs. Looks round. Something stinks. Not him. Flatface, probably. Flats don't wash much.

He looks up. A blue tube of grab-bar. Plenty strong enough. He reaches, puts his right by his left, uses both to haul his thin frame up as far as it'll go. Hangs, head brushing the light fitting. Looks down. The Gs swing him twenty degrees off the vertical, the shocker-shocks and track-angles tilt him to the door and away. It's like he's in one of those force diagrams, vectors, like they did in maths. Or was it science? Years ago. Months anyway.

He's flying, he's safe. Maths was pointless but he can see this and feel it. He's become a piece of maths. Likes that.

He looks down. People packed like canned anchovies find space and slither back into it, away from this swinging nutjob. One doesn't. He looks down at her. A dark-haired olive-skinned office-dressed girl. Woman. Staring up at him, amused rather than scared.

He feels like Tarzan, King of the Jungle. 'Me Tarzan, you

Jane,' he says, like you do when you swing over a smiling woman. 'Hey Flats,' he shouts, over a sudden roar of rails. 'See that? That's something!'

'Don't call me Flatface,' Flatface says.

'I didn't. But hey Flatface, look at her! I'm in love. Her name's Jane. I'm in love.'

'I'm not Jane,' she says. Her voice is deep. It carries well over the train's roaring whining screech. 'You're not Tarzan. And you're not in love.'

She turns her back.

He lowers his feet to the grooved floor, hands still on the bar. Feels a shiver. 'You're not Jane,' he says, hushed. 'Sorry.'

'You think you're something,' she says over her shoulder. 'Don't you. Well ...'

She turns to face him, steps past him. She's tall, maybe taller than he is. She reaches up to the bar, puts her hands next to his, pulls herself up, up to the ceiling. 'I'm not really dressed for this,' she says. 'Don't stare.'

'I'm not,' Banx says. He pulls himself up beside her.

The train goes round a corner. They both swing to the door, then to the front when the driver brakes. Their feet touch. He feels something, like he's suddenly made of jelly. They swing apart.

The crowd reshuffles to keep out of their space as they shift. Flatface has eyes that are glued to this woman.

'Hey Flats,' Banx says.

'Yeah?'

'Look out the window.'

'Eh?'

Banx glances from Flatface to the woman, back to Flatface.

'Oh,' Flatface says. And obeys.

The train stops.

'Down?' Banx says.

She nods. They lower themselves together, stand side by side. The doors hiss open.

'Er,' he says.

'Mmm?'

People get off. People get on. The doors start beeping. He doesn't let anyone come between them. A robot says, 'Please stand clear of the closing doors'.

'You're not Jane,' he says again. 'Who are you?'

She turns towards him. He can't meet her eye. He's afraid his longing will be written in neon across the roof of the carriage. Everyone will know. Including Flatface. And then where will he be?

Exposed.

Embarrassed.

Vulnerable.

Oh yes.

But if he doesn't look her in the eye, she'll think he's shifty. And that's not what he is. So he does. And is lost.

His life will never be the same, he knows. He thinks she knows the same about hers. Like the resultant in a vector diagram they'll move in a new direction. It'll be their life.

Their eyes are locked together.

He holds out a hand.

She takes it.

'Next stop?' he says. 'Off?'

She smiles. 'Hey,' she says, 'yeah.'

'I'm Banx.'

'Banx,' she says. 'Call me Jane again.'

Give and Forgive

I'D BE ABLE to move if I wanted to, I thought. But I didn't want to. All I wanted to do was lie still. So I did.

I've no idea where I am, how I got here, how long I've been here. Something must have happened. Do I even know my name? I wanted to say Bryan, with a 'Y'. That seemed to fit with Tollemarche Road, Birkenhead. And a postcode went with it, in my head. Enough for now. I felt so woozy.

I was lying on my back. I could feel footsteps through my skin before I could hear them. Two people, out of rhythm, one treading heavy and slow, the other lighter and faster. They were talking. A man and a woman. She called him 'Father', but not like he was her dad. He called her 'Nurse'. He had such a warm voice, you'd want to say yes to whatever he asked, however stupid it might be. He had an accent. Irish. Dublin, maybe. The best English in the world is spoken in Dublin, someone from Dublin once told me. Someone from Edinburgh said the same thing about Edinburgh. No-one'd say it about London, would they, with its ghastly Mockney glottal stops? Or Cardiff. Or Liverpool, where I might be now, from the way the nurse talks.

'Please do nothing to disturb him, Father,' she said. 'You can sit quietly, give him the unction, do you call it? Commendation? If you think that's necessary. I don't. But quietly, please.'

'Quietly, surely,' he said. 'Thank you.'

I heard footsteps going away. Hers. A rustle and creak as he settled into a chair. The smell of old man's aftershave.

Give and Forgive

Every ten seconds there was a two-second mechanical shush of something, some medical thing, beside me. The shush coincided with a cool tingle in the back of my left hand. Which I couldn't move. I couldn't move anything. Couldn't open my eyes. Speak. Sit up. And I wanted to now. I didn't know what unction and commendation were but they didn't sound like a lot of fun. I wanted to find out where I was and who these people were and get myself on my feet, but I couldn't lift a finger. I began to wonder why I wasn't scared.

'Let's say your death is close,' he said, quietly. 'An hour away. And, assuming you can hear me - I know you can't tell me, so don't try - but assuming you can...'

I heard him shift in his chair, unfold a piece of paper. I didn't like him.

'You've no doubt heard the Lord's Prayer,' he said. 'It's hard to avoid, whether or not you've had a Christian upbringing. But for most people it's just words spoken by rote. Not many interrogate its meaning.'

Another rustle and creak. He might have been crossing his legs.

'What it boils down to, I think, is this. Give and forgive. Give us our daily bread and forgive us our trespasses. Let us give to others. Let us forgive their trespasses against us. Give and forgive. I wonder whether that makes sense to you.'

He cleared his throat. Paper rustled.

'Can you be thinking about it?' he said. 'Right here, now. Who do you need to forgive?'

Whoever did this to me, I thought, whatever it is. Unless I did it to myself. Or was it one of those random accidents, like an oil spill across the road, just as you're leaning into a fast corner with a perfect camber? Which makes me think

I was on my bike when something happened. Bonneville T120. I love it. I forgive it, if it did wrong.

'You don't look like one of these people who go through life blaming their parents for what they've become,' he said.

He was right, I don't blame them. They fuck you up, your mum and dad, as someone said. But they don't mean to, and it's up to you to un-fuck yourself, isn't it?

'Brothers and sisters?' he said.

I have brothers. I like them. Nothing to forgive there. I just hope they forgive me. I was the oldest. And the biggest, for a while. I never meant to be cruel, but.

'Cruel playground bullies?' he said. 'Left far behind by now, and far away. And shafted by karma, to be sure.'

Was that it? Had I been shafted by karma? Odd turn of phrase for a priest, if that's what he was. But I'd been shafted by something, and there'd been times when I'd not been as kind as I should be. Like that thing at school with the cigarette lighter. I was beginning to see what he was getting at. Maybe it really was time to think about who I needed to forgive. Faces came clamouring out of the past.

That cool drug-dealing hipster who gave me a floor to sleep on when I had nothing. Who also routinely beat his beautiful damaged girlfriend, and I did nothing about it.

The biker who said he'd help repair my BSA Gold Star, then stole it, bit by bit, to fix his own. But I stole his girlfriend, then stupidly let her go. And his next girlfriend, ditto.

The ones whose words were worthless. Whose promises pleased, then evaporated.

The ones who died before their time, before I'd made the time for them. The best I've ever known.

'It seems possible you could die before your time,' he said, as if he could hear my thoughts. 'So you'd have any

Give and Forgive

amount of unfinished business. The less of that you take with you, the better. If you can find the soft touch of forgiveness in your soul, for any of those who wronged you, and for yourself... remember, we're all just people, doing what people do, trying to get through their day.'

His breath was slightly uneven, a bit of a catch to it, as if he might be unwell.

I found that soft touch somewhere, to my surprise. Found it quite easily. Felt it in waves, washing away bitterness and regret for what I'd done and left undone. For the dealer, whose girlfriend stayed with him to the end. For the biker, who meant well at the start. For Lin and Val, who I could have loved kinder. The one I most needed to forgive was me.

'I'm not going to mess around with wafers and wine,' he said, 'or any of that mumbo jumbo. And I see from your face that something's changed. So we'll get on with it while we can. I'll just give you the words, the important ones, without the flummery.'

He took a breath. The paper rustled.

'Eternal rest awaits you,' he said. 'Perpetual light shines on you, within you, and through you. Rest in peace. Rest in union with the light.'

I felt something at the centre of my forehead. His touch, oily. Anointment. The deep savoury smell of olives, comforting but sour.

'Forgive me, father,' he said, 'for I know not what I do.'

Something touched my lips.

His lips.

His lips touched my lips.

And stayed there. For much too long.

I didn't like it. And it felt weird. Inside I was exploding with alarm at the invasion of my space, but outside my body was just lying immobile and accepting. I couldn't even breathe at him.

Footsteps.

I felt them before I heard the door open.

He pulled away.

Someone came in.

The nurse.

'Father,' she hissed. She must have sensed something amiss.

'Nurse,' he said. 'I can explain.'

'Explain?' she said. 'Go on.'

He said nothing.

'You'd better leave,' she said. 'Now. And I'll be checking the webcam ...'

'Oh,' he said.

'And don't think I won't be reporting it, if there's anything untoward there. To your superiors. And to the police.'

I heard him scuffle out. The door close. A key turn in the lock.

I could tell she was still there.

'We'll not be disturbed now,' she said. I felt safe again.

She cleaned my forehead with a wet wipe. I like that fresh scent they have, synthesised chemical muck though it may be. She cleaned my face. My lips, where his lips had been. My neck. Wherever he'd trespassed.

Her touch was full of care. I felt so grateful.

I felt the bed shift. She sat beside me, took each of my hands in hers, squeezing firm but not hurting. She held them for a long time.

She leaned close. Her breath tickled my ear.

'You're cured,' she whispered.

I could see. Could I? Or imagine. I was seeing or imagining a small room. White walls. No window. One door. The nurse, all in white. Tall, dark, smiling.

I felt the pain pour in. I heard a long mournful moan. It came from my throat.

'Shush,' she said.

She put a finger to my lips and tip-toed away.

Everything was white.

Pulsing white.

Then whiter.

Set Out Running

HE'S NOT SNUGGED up into Sophie's warm back. He's not in bed. He's downstairs, on the sofa.

Last night comes back to him in a lump. It was no ordinary row. He can still taste its bitterness.

The dog whiffles under the dining table, curled in sleep. The Little Ben clock over the fireplace says quarter to four. Dawn's early light creeps through the curtains. He's had enough. Of the job. Of the city. Enough of their friends, who were all her friends anyway. Enough of being a family man, in this sort of family.

He dresses from the tumble dryer. Puts a change of clothes in a shoulder bag. Finds his jacket in the hall, checks his wallet: £120 in notes, some Euros. Driving licence, GHIC, bank cards. Gets into the banking app on his phone, moves one third of their savings to his personal account.

What else? Passport, middle drawer of the dresser. He crosses out Sophie as Emergency Contact, writes in his cousin in Stockport. In the same drawer, there's a document wallet, with 'CERTS' in her big black capitals on the front: he takes his HND Mech Eng, RYA Yachtmaster Offshore, Level 5 Dip of Ed & Training, St Johns First Aid At Work with CPR and Fire Marshal endorsements. Picks up his half-read book from the floor. Phone charger, notebook, pen. Toothbrush and toothpaste, from the downstairs bathroom. That's enough stuff.

He calls AZB taxis for a pick-up by the Spar on Manchester Road in ten minutes. Puts on well-worn boots:

cherry red, steel toecaps. Writes a note:

> *I've taken £2K from Lloyds to get started. Everything else is yours. You'll be happier without me. Loved you once. Good luck.*

Sticks it under the tea caddy, and takes a last look round at what was his life. Feels nothing except a need to be moving.

The taxi drops him outside Hallam University at four fifty. He crosses the road and walks to Sheffield rail station through curvy steel panels and sparkling fountains, feet so light he could skip. Buys tobacco, Rizlas and lighter from a newsagent, in case he takes up smoking again. Walks onto the station concourse. At five in the morning it's already hot and humid and busy: students with rucksacks, business people with laptops. The departures board refreshes, all the crowds rush to Platform 8, the London train. He's not going there.

So many places. Birmingham, Southampton, Cardiff, going south. Leeds, Newcastle, Edinburgh, going north. All too obvious. West looks better: Manchester, Liverpool. Or east. Lincoln, Hull.

He's never been to Hull.

He buys a one-way ticket.

Not many people going to Hull this morning. He has a table to himself, all the way. Talks to a ticket inspector from Rotherham, who used to drive buses. Reads his book. Loves the muddy ooze of the Humber, the arc of the suspension bridge. Doesn't look back once.

At half eight he's standing outside Hull Paragon station, on a wide street called Ferensway. It's full of small bikes and scooters delivering takeaway food. Who for? Who gets take-aways delivered for breakfast? He walks to the kerb, stops, looks both ways. There's sea salt in the air, a cool easterly drizzle. A short fat man stands on a corner, dressed as Spiderman, advertising pizzas. And another.

He walks south, towards the brightest patch of sky. Passes a business-like redbrick church. An ice rink boarded up. Another fat Spiderman. A sign on a post says Trans-Pennine Long-Distance Footpath, which sounds unlikely, here by the sea. He follows where it points, down a narrow alley between high chain-link fences, onto a deserted dockside. A board swinging loose on a gate says 'Albert Dock'.

To his right, five big cargo boats lie alongside in a floating harbour. Orange hulls, grey superstructure, no people. To the left, the biggest lock he's ever seen, and a Portakabin. Beyond them, the Humber estuary and the North Sea.

It's peaceful here. He stops and breathes deep, thinks about what he's done, whether he had a choice. And what he's going to do. Plenty of choices there. Go back to engineering or teaching. Write something. Join a band. Take art seriously. Starve in a garret. Work in a factory, shop, distribution centre. Advertise pizzas. No rush though. He set out running but will take his time.

He leans on a post a few yards from the Portakabin, trying to feel the sun, smelling fish, watching gulls clean up. He wishes he still smoked, realises he can. Rolls up, sucks it down, his head instantly spinning. He flicks the half-smoked butt into the lock, making a ripple in still water. Mullet cruise over. One sucks the butt in, blows it out again. And another. It must look like food to them.

You can't trust looks. Everyone knows that. But little Patrick, two weeks old, fit as a fiddle, with orange hair and freckles - the child doesn't look like him at all. Never will. Maybe you can't trust looks. But you can trust a DNA test.

A stubby bloke crops up behind him, asks for a light.

Set Out Running

'Sure,' he says.

The bloke blows out a cloud, stands back a foot or two, but hangs around, like he's waiting for something.

More people come down the path from town, and stand in line behind the stubby one. Men with bags over their shoulders, papers in their hands.

He's in a queue. In fact he's the front of a queue, and looking the part, with his bag and his boots.

A man half-way back looks at his watch. They all do. He does. It's nine o'clock. A door opens in the Portakabin, a man looks out, beckons. Grey stubble, tanned, white shirt with black epaulettes. Beckons him, as the man at the front of the queue. He walks over. He can't help smiling.

At ten past nine he's out on the dock with three pieces of paper and a wide grin. What a nice bloke that was. Robbie Suggett. Robbie gave him the papers, three small black and white miracles. A room for a week, in the seaman's hostel. Enrolment for a four-day course, ABS Deck Certificate. And a contract. Trainee deckhand, on the SS Tijndrum, one of those orange-hulled freighters in Albert Dock. Sailing next Friday.

He's never been to the Baltic.

Why Don't We Find Out?

WHEN I WAS twenty, I played guitar in an acid rock/ska fusion band steeped in hippy ideals of universal love and compassion. The other guitarist was a gentle man from the Scots borders called Ewan. Mystic Kev was the drummer. Bassists came and went. We were into a kind of disciplined jamming, riffing around our own songs and re-imagined covers.

One song we wrote together, *'Do you still think of me?'*, was about love we'd lost that still haunted our hearts. Each of us had one. Mine was Melissa. The song had a ska rhythm, three verses that we wrote together, and a middle eight that was all mine.

The middle eight went:
Do you remember that April night, by the bus-stop under the light?
The words go around in my head, when I think of how you said
'We might not even be sexually compatible'
and I said 'It looks like we'll never find out'
and we didn't. We never found out.

Every word of that was true, except it was September, but April scanned better. I was seventeen when it happened, still a child, officially. But Mel and I had just left school, and thought we were grown up.

* * *

Three years later, the band was playing *'Do you still think?'* for the hundredth time, at a gig in Carlisle, the High School's summer ball. The opening riff had a chunky metro-Caribbean beat. It went on as long as we wanted. I was in my place, out front, stage right. I chugged away on my Strat, looking out at all these kids grooving, dancing, holding each other, laughing. Seventeen or eighteen years old, they looked so young. Most of them would be leaving school right after this end-of-term do. Most of them would be losing their own sweet first loves, whether they knew it now or not. And I started sobbing. I had to stop playing, tears streaming. Because it had just occurred to me what Mel had meant, stupid man that I am; and what I should have said, three years ago, which definitely wasn't, 'It looks like we'll never find out'.

Ewan was the sensitive one. He was at stage left, opposite me, on his lovely hollow-bodied Gibson, cherry red, f-holes. Our guitars had to talk to each other, it was the point of how we played. Ewan didn't know what was going on with me, but he knew something was. He hit a long mean note, and let it float. Kev picked something up through his hippy haze, and started blasting round-the-house drum rolls, louder and louder. With each blast from Kev, Winged-Eel Winston slid from bottom to top of his fretless bass, and it hung and it hung until I came back into the beat and we were off like a runaway train. We never played that song better.

* * *

I met Mel when I was thirteen. I couldn't take my eyes off her face, but all we did was look at each other across rows of desks. Boys never sat with girls, or spent time with them at break. I went to her place once, when I was fifteen, a long bus journey and a three mile walk on a busy road to this big detached house on the edge of a village. I hadn't been invited. Her mother answered the door. I'd never met her but she seemed to know who I was. I overcame utter tongue-tied-ness and said, 'Is Mel in?'

She looked at me like you'd look at a slug in your salad, and said, 'I'm not having my daughter mixing with your type'. Then closed the door firmly and turned the key in the lock.

I walked back down their drive to the road, and all the long way home I felt more slug than human.

* * *

I tried to sit near Mel on school trips. We hugged and kissed once, on a dark coach coming back from something worthy in Sheffield. Antigone, or the Hallé doing Beethoven. Then we left school. I spent that summer as I usually did, working on a farm in the White Peak. I needed to save for a gap year in Europe, so worked non-stop. I went home in September, the day before Mel had to leave for Manchester to start her teacher training. We had our one and only actual date that evening. She told her parents she was going to visit her friend Anne in Bolsover.

I met her off the bus and we spent two hours together. We went to the Blue Bell Inn. I paid for a Babycham and half of bitter. My hands were shaking. Neither of us had a clue what to do or how to do it. It was a strange, strained evening.

She had to be home by nine. I walked her to the bus-stop, an awkward arm round her shoulders. We had a stilted talk, waiting for the bus, under the light. It was a time when international phone calls had to be booked and placed through an operator, long before mobiles. We promised to write often, to keep in touch, and to see each other as soon as we could, which would be the following July. And then that exchange, as her bus appeared in the distance:

She: *We might not even be sexually compatible.*
Me: *It looks like we'll never find out.*

The bus pulled up. I went to kiss her, missed her lips. She looked at me like I was an idiot, then was gone.

* * *

June, ten months later, I was back in the UK, on the Men's Medical ward at Mansfield General Hospital, with a fever that was diagnosed and treated as rheumatic but which turned out to be glandular. I was still there at the end of July, still couldn't really walk. I'd not spoken to Mel since she got on that bus in Bolsover. I'd not heard from her since a postcard at Easter. I guessed she'd be back at her parents' house for the summer. As soon as I could sit up and talk, I wanted to see her.

In the hospital you could book a phone call. They'd bring a handset and plug it in to a socket on the wall, behind the bed. You'd be in the middle of the ward, idle ears all round you, eager for distraction. Much too public for the sort of conversation I wanted to have. I felt so nervous each time I rang, and I had to keep trying until it wasn't her mother that answered. When I finally got Mel, she sounded surprised to hear from me, shocked. She'd come in and visit the next day.

I'd never wanted anyone else. We were made for each other, and now we were both eighteen and adult, I was convinced we'd finally be together. I knew it was what we both longed for. I'd been debating whether to pop the question as soon as I saw her, but I was still unwell, and the docs couldn't tell me when or even whether I'd ever be properly fit again. So I was thinking maybe I should hold off, until I was out of hospital. But maybe not. I couldn't decide.

Visiting hour. Mel walked in among a crowd of visitors, looked round. She seemed grown-up and nervous and happy. I was half-way out of bed in my PJs, reaching out to hug her.

'Did you get my letter?' she said, backing off.

'What letter?'

She held out her left hand. A ring on the third finger, a narrow band, a solitaire diamond. She was engaged.

'Oh God, you don't know, do you? I explained, in my letter. Oh God. Well, you know now.' She sat by the bed, showed me a photo of a big blond Viking type from Blackburn, proud. You can take all the break-up songs ever written, put them in a big brown pot and still them down to a dram of purest misery, and you'd not come close to the poison I had to swallow while I tried to look pleased for her.

* * *

I thought about her on and off over the years, but never tried to get in touch. Until I did.

I've always loved long-distance walking. On my own of course, I couldn't cope with someone blethering on beside me, day in, day out. Since my marriage broke up and my ex took off with our daughter, I was doing a lot of it. At the end of May I was on the West Highland Way, heading north from Glasgow. It rained from Drymen to Doune Byre bothy at the north end of Lomond. Thirty bloody miserable muddy miles.

I was so glad to walk out of the cold wet and into shelter. It was full of a humid fug and hearty hiking types singing Hey Ho the Raglan Bog and all that jazz. And there in the

Why Don't We Find Out?

midst of the fun was this guy with a vacant smile and ears like Dumbo's, shining red in the candle-light. I'd have known him anywhere: Mel's big brother Greg, part of the hearty party, who were doing an east-west route from Callander in Perthshire to Machrihanis on Kintyre. Typically ambitious, practically uncharted.

He and I got talking. He was an innocent abroad, just as bland as I remembered him. Mel was all we had in common. I told him how I was newly free and single, plied him with my emergency reserve of Highland Park, and quizzed him about Mel's life. Subtly, of course. He told me where she was working (a school in Warrington), how many children she had (three), and how she was deeply unhappy with her husband (Roger the Viking). Apparently he actually hit her. Some kind of caveman.

We went our ways the next morning, promising to stay in touch, like you do. And I couldn't stop thinking about her. How she'd been when we were young. How she might be now. Did she still think of me?

So I wrote a letter, marked private and confidential, posted to her school. She wrote back. And I wrote back to her, and so on. And it turned out that she did still think of me, and was all through with the Viking, in principle, though still living with him, and was all for getting together with me. I was surprised, it seemed a bit of a leap, especially with three kids in tow, but I was seriously interested, as you would be, despite being a bit apprehensive about over-committing up front, and more than a bit dubious about why she was still with him if he was such an ass. I'd not seen her for nearly twenty years, and it didn't seem like either of us had a great track record on relationships. But we exchanged more letters, and had a surreptitious phone call or two. One thing led to another, and I booked a room in a hotel just outside

Tarporley in Cheshire, and drove up from Oxford to meet her for lunch.

I couldn't stop thinking, all the way there, that we might not even be sexually compatible.

We met in the hotel car park. I checked in. We skipped lunch, went up to our room. Talked awkwardly for about ten seconds, then found out.

We weren't.

It wasn't that she wasn't attractive – she was.

It wasn't that sex was impossible. It was more that it felt strange and wrong. More like fucking a complete stranger than doing something joyous with the love of your life. And I don't know how to put this any other way - it just didn't smell right.

I drove back south, thinking about what sexual compatibility could mean, and how life might have been easier for both of us if I'd said, that night at the bus-stop, 'Why don't we find out?' Or if she had. Though she probably thought she'd said enough.

I wrote her another letter:

Thanks for trying. Sorry. It's not going to work for me.

No reply.

* * *

Five years later, life was in one of its transitional phases. I had just wrapped up a twenty-odd year career in software design, and was about to start an MSc in social research methods. Things had settled down with my ex. I saw my daughter regularly. I had finally met the woman I wanted to spend the rest of my days with, and, god willing, we were getting married in the autumn. Life was busy, and the future felt full of good things.

Why Don't We Find Out?

It was the last weekend of the school summer holidays. Most Saturday mornings we had some sort of outing, usually a picnic and dog-walk on Port Meadow if the weather was okay. Normally friends joined us, so there were often three or four adults and their children, all bringing things to eat and to feed the ducks.

This morning the weather was fine, the picnic was organised, and I was heading down the hall with bags and bottles and dog and daughter when the door-bell rang. I dropped my bags, opened the door and looked out. A woman stood there, the sun bright behind her, turned half away from me. A car was parked on the street, with driver's door open and another older woman in the passenger seat.

'Can I help you?' I said.

The woman at the door turned to the woman in the car and said, 'He doesn't even recognise me.'

I was doing a double take. Who was she?

She turned back to me. It was Mel. The woman in the car must be her mother. My mouth opened but nothing came out.

'You're getting married,' she said, as if it was the ultimate betrayal.

How did she know?

'Yes.'

She walked to the car, got in, drove away.

Epilogue

I exchange Christmas messages with Ewan, and clips of music. He still plays, but became something of a celebrity for other good reasons.

Drummer Kev died, in Africa, in his west-coast hotel that had become a centre for world music. He was a lion of a man.

At least two of the bassists are still trucking on, in their own ways, and still making music.

I do the odd open mike night, but don't play a lot these days, being more into writing, and too old and deaf for rock and roll. I'm still married, and will stay that way, god willing.

I heard that Mel is still with her Viking. She's probably a grandmother now.

I hope she's okay.

The Tide Turned

A CRESCENT MOON was rising between tower blocks. Or possibly setting. I sat on a bench, by the canal, at the end of my second year at Manchester Metropolitan. I had toothbrush, trunks, towel and a change of clothes in a backpack. £30 in a pocket. I had to get away, wasn't sure I'd ever come back. I wanted sun, blue skies, salt water. And romance, of course. If possible.

I hoisted my pack, walked into the bus station. A bored woman at the booking desk said, 'Can I help you?'

'I need to get to the seaside. Somewhere I can find work.'

'Where?'

'Where is there?'

She pushed across a book of timetables, well-thumbed. It was open at the Bs. I skimmed through. Basingstoke. Bath. Bedford. Berwick. Bicester. Birmingham. Blackburn. Bletchley. Blyth. Bodmin. Bognor Regis.

Bognor's on the coast. There must be jobs. I bought a one-way ticket.

* * *

The following morning, outside Bognor bus station, I found a newsagent's window full of ads. One said:

Seasonal workers wanted. £86 a week plus room and board. Full training given.

I phoned up and they said yes, sight unseen. I started

The Tide Turned

my first shift that afternoon, as a short order chef in the KwikSnak café, on the Butlins holiday camp. Six days a week and on the seventh you rested. I worked the late shift, 4 p.m. to somewhere between midnight and 1 a.m.

I didn't mind the cooking, got quite good at it. Hated almost everything else. But when I came off shift I always went down to the shingle beach to swim. Cold salt water on my skin washed away the cooking oil and made me feel alive again. It was the best part of the day.

Barney told me that Billy Butlin got his start buying up surplus PoW camps after WWII. It made sense. Chalets for happy campers were like tarted up cell blocks. Staff accommodation wasn't tarted up at all. I shared a room with Barney, on the third floor of Block H. He was from Darlington. He had the top bunk. He'd had the room to himself until I turned up. He'd have preferred it to stay that way.

Barney had shoulder-length blond hair, Jagger lips, cheeks like skin-on chicken breasts, pouty and goose-bumped. He laughed wildly at anything anyone said, himself included, funny or not, even if it was like, 'I've got a headache'. He was a redcoat, an entertainer, an aristocrat in the camp hierarchy. But unlike most redcoats he didn't actually wear a red coat. He spent most of his working days dressed as a giant cockerel, strutting around, crowing at terrified children.

He thought he was some kind of rock star. And though I couldn't see it, Barney had something that some women found attractive. Half the time he spent his nights elsewhere, but if he came back to the room he always had a woman with him. Never the same one. It didn't bother him that I was trying to sleep in the bunk below. God knows what the women thought, if they even knew I was there.

* * *

One Saturday night at the end of August I had my swim and went back to the room. 2 a.m., still empty. I said my prayers and went to bed. I was deep asleep when Barney pitched up, with friend. I opened an eye. She was slight, dark-haired, not his usual substantial blonde type. I turned to the wall and did my best to see no evil, hear no evil. And to suppress a sneeze.

Barney barged into bunks and lockers, drunk as usual, but got the two of them up on the top bunk eventually, and something like a wrestling match began. It started with creaks and twangs. Barney would whisper *Come on* and she'd hiss *No* or *Please don't* or *Not there* in reply and the dialogue built up in pace and volume and didn't exactly sound consensual. I was weighing up how to intervene without starting world war three when she shouted, 'Stop! Now! Let me go!' and I sneezed as loud as I've ever sneezed and she screamed and Barney spewed his evening's intake over everything: the poor girl, the bunks, the wall, the bedside cabinet, the concrete floor, me.

I reached out and hit the slimy light switch. Ghastly threads dripped past my face. It smelled awful. 'For Christ's sake, Barney,' I said, shucking out of bed, backing off across the room.

'Yes, for Christ's sake, Barney,' the girl said, looking at me wide-eyed, sitting on the edge of the top bunk. I started laughing and couldn't stop. She said, 'It's not funny,' and started laughing too. She wiped her face with her sleeve, said 'Ugh', held out an arm.

I helped her slide down to the floor. She had brown eyes. She could have been pretty, in different circumstances.

Barney started snoring. I stopped laughing, tried for a

The Tide Turned

sympathetic smile.

'For Christ's sake,' she said again, shaking her head at Barney, turning to me. 'You were very quiet. I didn't know anyone was down there.'

'What did you want me to do? Commentate? Hum along?'

'Don't be sarky, it doesn't suit you.'

I wasn't going to argue about how she knew what did and didn't suit me. I dug around in my locker, handed her a towel. Picked up another. Stuffed my feet into trainers, headed out the door. 'Come along,' I said.

'Where?'

'The sea! The sea!'

'That's the name of a book,' she said.

'Yes. Iris Murdoch,' I said, pausing in the corridor. 'It starts with someone looking at the sea. Which is glowing in the sun, rather than sparkling. She says the sea leans against the land when the tide turns. Quietly. Something like that.'

'Leans against the land. That's nice. Did you just know that?'

'Did it for A level,' I said.

'Let's see for ourselves,' she said.

I breathed easier having left Barney behind. We went carefully down the stairs in the dim light, walked side by side through the camp gates, past the sleeping security men, and across the promenade and out onto the shore. We dropped the towels on the shingle and ran into the water in whatever we were wearing. Swam out a good way through a gentle swell, side by side. Stopped, lying back on the waves, arms spread, heads back, watching the Milky Way.

'That's Orion,' I said, pointing, breaking a long silence. 'The big one at the top is a red giant. Betelgeuse.'

She was quiet.

'Down there's Rigel,' I said. 'It's supposed to be blue. The bright one down right is Sirius, his dog, the dog star. And that little slant across the middle …'

She snorted.

'… is his belt,' I said.

'The Greeks said it was his willy.'

I wanted to be clever-clogs and say something that wasn't very funny, but thought better of it.

'At least it would be,' she said, 'if it was Orion. But it's Lyra. Orion won't show up for a few weeks yet.'

A meteor slid across the sky. Was it buzzing?

'Wish upon a star,' she said, holding out her right hand. 'I'm Suzie. From Sutton. In Ashfield, not Surrey. My brother's got a six-inch reflector.'

'That's a telescope,' I said. I took her hand. We floated in a slow circle. 'I'm Jack. I'm not from anywhere much. Manchester I suppose, these days. A bit lost really.'

'Aren't we all,' she said.

I couldn't believe how easy it felt, how comfortable. I was with a woman and I wasn't nervous. I'd never felt anything like it. Was this love?

I kept my mouth shut, it seemed the wisest thing. We swam slowly back to shore, lay on our towels on the shingle.

'So what was going on back there?' I said. 'Why were you with Barney?'

'Jack. That's a question.'

'It is.'

'I guess you've a right to ask.'

'I knew I shouldn't,' I said. 'It just came out.'

'How much do you know about women, Jack? Their sexuality.'

I couldn't really say I knew loads, could I? Because I didn't. 'Not a lot, really,' I said. 'I've had a few girlfriends.

None that lasted.'

'But you must know about men. You know that men sometimes just want sex. No strings, no commitment, no chat ...'

'Well yes.'

'Women are just the same.'

'Oh,' I said. 'Crikey. I hadn't actually ... I didn't really ... '

'That's why I was with Barney. Can we stop talking about that now? And before you ask ...'

'I wasn't going to. I know. You're not feeling that way anymore. You've moved on.'

I put an arm out.

We wrapped around each other.

She slept.

The tide crept ever more slowly up the shingle, then paused twenty feet away. It felt like the mass of the whole world's water was leaning against the shore right there, quietly waiting for the earth to turn.

Lit by the new moon, the sea glowed like pearl.

Party Wall

Dulcie was still in her dressing gown. She had her back to the wall, between the dresser and the corner cupboard. A dark woman in police uniform was sitting in Dulcie's chair. A man sat in my chair, older than the woman. He had a deep tan and short grey hair, and was dressed more for mountain walking than the dull suburbs of a southern city. 'Mr Williams,' he said. He was Scottish. He spoke softly, but we could all hear him. 'I'm Detective Sergeant Grant. This is PC Dodds. How did you sleep?'

I looked at him. Usually a simple 'Fine, thanks' or 'Not too bad' will suffice, but sometimes someone really wants to know, like if they're a nurse, or a doctor. Or, as now, a policeman.

'Why do you ask?' I said

He looked back at me, sighed. 'I'll explain later,' he said.

I'd no idea why they were here. Dulcie had shouted 'Albert, visitors', and I'd come straight downstairs in my dressing gown. I'd had an awful night, as it happened. My head felt like it had been kicked by a donkey. I wasn't too pleased to be dragged down and questioned about how I'd slept. And my chair was occupied, and Dulcie's. So I stood by the table and decided to give him a full account.

'Badly,' I said. 'For a start we were late getting back from the cricket in Nottingham. Play finished at half six and the traffic was terrible. It was too late to cook and we were tired, so we rang ahead and booked a table at the Standard, in Jericho. Always nice there. We had a drop of Kingfisher, it's perfect with a curry. Home by eleven. Dulcie went straight to bed. I did the crossword, had a small whisky. A few pistachios. Liquorice. Dark chocolate. I gave up smoking twenty-odd years ago, but …'

Constable Dodds carried on scribbling in a notebook for several seconds.

'Am I giving you too much detail?' I asked her, feeling certain I was.

She stopped with pencil poised, smiled, shook her head.

Grant said, 'You're fine, carry on. Talk us through the timeline.'

'Okay. By half twelve I was nodding off in my chair. Which is that one,' I said to Grant. 'The one you're sitting in.'

He didn't move, so I took a dining chair by the table and carried on. 'I made a valerian tea, took it up, crept into bed. Dulcie was out for the count. I went straight to sleep. I should have known better. Eating so late doesn't suit me, and then with the scotch and nibbles … I was awake again at three with acid reflux, horrible. But a quick gargle and a slug of gripe water …'

'Gripe water?' Grant said.

'Yes. Nurse Hardy's. Meant for babies, but I swear by it. I once met a chap called Arthur who'd inherited the Nurse Hardy's Gripe Water fortune. You'd not think there'd be big money in gripe water, but there must have been, once. He was from Leeds. Came on like an aristocrat, lived like one too. Spent his whole life fishing for salmon. Bastard. Anyway, a good swallow of that and a few deep breaths of fresh air and I could try sleeping again, propped up on three pillows. I woke at five and went down to two pillows. And at half six, down to my normal one pillow. Woke again at eight, when Dulcie brought tea.' I nodded at her. She was half hidden behind the dresser, looking anxious about something, but not volunteering any information. She's not usually the nervous type. Was something serious was going on?

They seemed to want the detail on how I'd slept before they told me anything, so I carried on. 'The tea was cold when I went to pick it up. I saw it was nine o'clock, and I was just going to ask Dulcie to bring another when she called up to say we had visitors. I came down and there you were.'

A lot of information but PC Dodds had apparently written it all down, so it can't have been too much. DS Grant just listened, watching me, which I found disconcerting. They wouldn't be doing research on sleeping habits, would they? So were they collecting evidence? Of what?

Grant said, 'What woke you at three o'clock?'

'This blasted reflux business,' I said.

'Was your wife awake?'

'Not that I noticed.'

'What kind of night was it?'

'It was dark,' I said.

'Talk us through what you did at three o'clock.'

I'd not been fully awake at the time, and I wasn't fully awake now, so the memories came back piece by piece. 'I went to the bathroom for gripe water. Looked out the back. Chewed a Rennie. Opened the window, did a bit of deep breathing. It was very dark. No moon. But not cloudy.'

I took a deep breath. Things were coming back to me. 'There was a strong smell when I opened the window,' I said, 'like new-mown hay. But that's unlikely, isn't it, in May? There were stars, but you couldn't see many, because of the orange glow, over the city. And I heard an owl. Tawny. Soliciting.'

'An owl?'

'Ker-wick. Or Tu-Whit, in the vernacular.'

'Soliciting?'

'You're right, it's odd. It's sometimes hard to tell where a sound comes from, in the dark. But I remember thinking it must be close, like in next door's garden, the Bonners. I was at the window of the spare room, next to the bathroom.' I pointed up and across.

'It sounded loud, like it was in the bushes the other side of their fence.' I pointed again, through the conservatory doors. 'Close. And low down. But owls usually call from high up. And it's summer, isn't it? Nearly. They can make that call any time, but it's a mating call. The female's. Or a territory call, if it's much repeated. You'd hear it most in the autumn, winter, through into spring. Now, late May, you'd expect more pulsed hooting, round the nest. So that's odd too. Anyway it shut up when Randolph went out. Randolph Bonner that is, the neighbour on that side.'

I looked round for Dulcie. She'd wedged herself into the corner, still in her dressing gown, with a tea towel in her hand, twisting it up like she was wringing it out. She was looking at me as if there was something she needed to tell me but didn't feel able to. Not like her to hold back. Perhaps it was the presence of the plods.

PC Dodds stopped writing. She looked at me, and Grant leaned forward and looked at me too. It felt quite intense. What had I said?

Dulcie could do with a break, I thought. I'd been rattling on, and I don't usually say a word in the morning until I've had two good strong mugs of tea. So I said, 'Can you get us all a nice cup of tea, dear? Or me at least, I'm parched.' But she just frowned and looked down and raised her eyes to me again.

'Mr Bonner went out?' Grant said.

'He went down the garden, and came back with a barrow. I remember thinking, what a funny time to be fetching a wheelbarrow up the garden. And then that relation of hers. Her cousin, is it? You remember, Dulcie, the noisy one that was so rude that day, not long after they moved in?'

Dulcie nodded.

'That one. Bald. Mouthy. Anyway he came up the garden with Randolph. The cousin had a spade in each hand. Or a shovel in one hand and a spade in the other, I couldn't be sure.'

'You could see all that, in the dark?'

'Yes. They'd left lights on inside.'

Grant glanced at PC Dodds, nodded. 'So Randolph Bonner went out, and came back with an empty wheelbarrow? And his wife's cousin didn't go down with him, but followed him back carrying spades?'

'Yes,' I said. 'That's right.'

'And then?'

'Well nothing really. They went out of sight, behind their extension. Which doesn't half stick out a long way. We objected when they put in for planning. Made no difference,' I said. 'Then I went back to bed. With three pillows. As I was saying.'

Grant patted his pockets, frowned. 'The owl, Mr Williams. Was it definitely a real owl? Or could it have been somebody imitating an owl?'

'It sounded like an owl, but it was low down, close to the house. And it was repeated, like a territory call. But it's May. So I don't think it was an owl. On the balance of probabilities, as they say. A good imitation though.'

'Why might someone be imitating an owl in next door's garden at three in the morning?' Grant said. 'Any ideas?'

Party Wall

'No.' But I thought of children's stories. The Famous Five. Swallows and Amazons. 'A signal?' I said.

'Yes, possibly,' Grant said. 'Just to recap. There was hooting. Mr Bonner went out. He and the cousin came back, with implements. Yes?'

'Yes.'

'Thank you, ' Grant said.

I let out a breath that I hadn't realised I was holding. Everyone seemed to relax.

Grant turned to my wife. 'Mrs Williams. Dulcie. Thank you for calling us. You did the right thing. PC Dodds?'

I hadn't realised they were here because she'd called them.

'Yes,' PC Dodds said, consulting some notes. 'Can we just recap what you said when you called?'

Dulcie nodded, and stood straighter. She gave me a look that said it was her turn now. I relaxed a notch.

'You'd heard a row going on next door, from around midnight, with the man shouting and the child crying,' Dodds said. 'Which happens frequently, and is clearly audible through the party wall. And the wife, Cordilla, was joining in, which you say is less frequent.'

Dulcie nodded.

'Speak, please,' PC Dodds said.

'Yes,' Dulcie said. 'That's right.'

'You said it sounded like the wife was taking the child's side, trying to calm her husband down, stop him shouting at the child.'

Dulcie nodded again. 'Exactly, yes.'

'And then?'

'Around two thirty,' she said, 'it reached its loudest. There were some loud bangs. Then it all went quiet, until my husband woke up with his reflux.'

So Dulcie was awake then too. I hadn't noticed.

'And this morning?' Dodds said.

'There was a right to-do,' Dulcie said, 'involving Mr Bonner and the cousin. But I couldn't hear the mother or the child.'

Dodds nodded. 'What time was that?' she said.

'Seven thirty. The news had just started, on the radio.'

'Thank you.' Dodds made a note and nodded to Grant.

'Mr Williams,' Grant said, 'can we just pop upstairs and have a look out that window?'

We went up to the spare room. I wondered what he was expecting to see. I keep binoculars there, for watching birds. We always have lots nesting around the garden.

'May I?' Grant said, indicating the binoculars.

'Of course.'

He picked them up, removed the lens covers, looked down into our garden and next door's, adjusted the focus. 'Have a wee look at that,' he said. 'Beneath that tree, next door. Bottom of their garden. Old apple tree, is it?'

'It is,' I said. 'This whole area was orchard, before the houses were built. That was in the days when builders showed trees some respect. So lots of the gardens have an old apple. Ours is cookers. Theirs is eaters.'

PC Dodds was behind us, scribbling away again.

'See anything unusual, under the tree?'

'Someone's been digging there,' I said. 'That's new. It's always been just lawn, that part of their garden. I keep telling him he should leave it wilder, for insects and birds and small mammals, but he likes it neat and tidy. He's not dug it before. Stupid place to plant anything though.'

'Why?'

'Well, all the tree roots. And anything you plant there will get no light, will it? Because of the tree.'

Party Wall

We left the window, went down the stairs.

'PC Dodds,' Grant said, 'back to the car please. Keep an eye. Make sure no-one comes or goes. Call up the wagon and SOCOs and some youngsters to do the needful. They'll need to bring spades. Be with you in a sec, and we'll pop round for a word.'

Dodds left. Grant turned to me and Dulcie. 'Thank you for coming forward,' he said. 'We'll see what's what, next door. If necessary we'll have statements typed up and bring them over for you to check and sign. I'll leave you to your tea. Best not discuss this with anyone else for now, okay?'

Dulcie nodded, headed for the kettle.

'And Mr Williams,' Grant said. 'That stuff for reflux. Nurse Hardy's, you said?'

'That's right. You suffer too?' I said.

'Yes. Horrid, isn't it.'

Ridiculous

Mr Jarman, come in, sit down. This machine is recording our conversation. You do not have to say anything. But it may harm your defence if you do not mention when questioned something which you later rely on in court. Anything you do say may be given in evidence. Do you understand?

Yeah, sure.

I'm Detective Sergeant Grant, Thames Valley Police, Kidlington. Constable Dodds is also present. This is recording reference SPA-240729-00035. It's 3:40 a.m., Monday July 29th. Please state your name and address.

Kenneth Jarman. 58 Redwood Drive, Botley.

You know you're entitled to legal representation. Do you want that?

No I don't. Why should I?

Because you appear to have killed someone.

It was self-defence.

So you say. You're sure you don't want legal representation?

I don't, I just said.

Okay. You said earlier you've not been living at that address recently.

No, I haven't.

So where ...?

I've been living at the station. Sleeping on a bench. No-one seemed to care. Other dossers get moved on, but not me. With all the strikes, there's always people who've turned up for trains that didn't run, so I wasn't the only one hanging around. And my bench was out of the way. No-one else used it. And I didn't look like a dosser, I dressed okay, had my stuff in a nice bag, from John Lewis. And I kept myself clean. Washed, shaved, clean clothes.

How did you manage that?

The laundromat, for clothes. Up Botley Road. To change and clean up, I got on a train, so I could do it in the loo. Went somewhere, came back. If someone comes asking for tickets, you just look the other way.

Why were you sleeping on the station?

I thought that if I kept away from the house for a while, it'd give up and go away.

It?

Whatever it was that was stalking me or haunting me or...

What did this 'it' do? How did it manifest?

Noises in the house. Creaks, bangs. Windows open that I knew I'd shut. Bottles empty, that I knew had been full. Or I'd come down and find the hot water tap running. Or the fridge door open. Gas rings on. Windows steamed up. I thought if I went away for a week or so, the house might start behaving itself again, and I'd be able to sleep and get on with work and that.

Your work is ...?

Writing.

Writing what?

Fiction mostly. Three novels. Short stories, I've lost count. Over a hundred. The odd magazine article. Blogs. Press. I doubt you'd have read any though.

Full time, is it?

Yes, in that I don't do anything else. Never have. Never had time for anything else.

Been doing it long?

Since I left college, so fifteen ... no, twenty years. Twenty-odd. But google my name, you won't find much. Nothing, really. Except a magazine that I started, with a mate from uni. A sort of on-line thing.

You have an agent? Publisher?

I've been close to getting an agent. For one of the novels. And to having a story accepted. And there's been interest in articles and comment pieces. But I don't know. My wife used to say my writing's so far ahead of the curve that no-one'll get it for another decade. I don't know.

So how much do you earn from writing?

Not much.

So how much, say last tax year?

Well. Nothing, really.

Nothing at all?

Nothing.

How long did you sleep on the station?

About a week.

Did you go back to the house at all, in that time?

Not until this afternoon. Then I decided to check it out. I left my bag in a locker at the station. The house looked okay when I got there. The lawn needs a trim. Car's still there.

You walked ...?

Yeah, up the Botley Road, Westminster Way, second right, left into Redwood Drive. From the turning, I walked up opposite the house, on the odd numbers side, to the top of the hill, then back down on the even side, right past the house, just having a look. Didn't meet anyone.

What time was this?

Four, four-thirty?

What were you intending?

Just to have a look, make sure it still looked okay from the outside. I wasn't going to go in until tomorrow. But just when I was passing the house a light came on in the front bedroom.

Was that your bedroom?

No, I've always slept at the back. When we were sleeping together, we slept at the back. Then the front room became hers. Because of her shifts.

So the light?

I was surprised. I'd set up lights on timers all around the house, so it wouldn't look unoccupied. Going on and off at different times through the evening. But nothing should have been coming on then. I thought maybe there'd been a power cut, so all the timers would need adjusting. I was about to go in and check then I saw the old bloke at number sixty looking at me from his window. Next door, down the hill. He sort of pointed, like he had something to tell me. But he's a nosey bugger. I didn't want to talk to him. So I kept walking, brisk-ish. And decided to come back after supper.

Why?

To check the light out?

Where did you eat?

Luigi's. Frideswide Square, by the station. I had lasagne, if you want to know. Crème brûlée. Wine. Cognac. Coffee. They know me, I go quite often. I was a bit fed up with sleeping on the station, to be honest. Didn't seem a very attractive prospect. Thought I might try a night in the house, if it felt okay. So I got my bag, walked back. Got to the house about half ten, in the dark. No light in the front bedroom. A few on inside, but there should have been. I let myself in, it all seemed fine, the timers were all set right. So the only weird thing was, why had that light come on in the afternoon? I thought maybe I'd imagined it, because honestly, everything was exactly as I'd left it. I didn't go up and unpack, because I thought I might still go back to the station. While I thought about it I got my book out and found a bottle of Courvoisier. Poured a good one, with a splash of Saint-Géron.

What's that?

Water.

What book were you reading?

No Final Solution. Douglas Skelton.

That's about unsolved murders in Scotland.

It is. So I had a couple and read a bit and must have fallen asleep, on the sofa, in the front room. Curtains closed, just a reading light on. Don't know what woke me. Something. Then I was awake and listening. A bit nervous to be honest. Of course I didn't think it could be my wife, whatever else it was.

Your wife?

Ex-wife, sorry. Because she was in clink. HMP Bronzefield. Near junction 13 on the M25. Know it?

Yes. Go on.

Then there was this crash, upstairs. I jumped out of my skin. I was quite spooked. Got the Glock out of the fridge.

Glock?

Glock 17. I checked it was loaded, took the safety off.

That's a serious weapon. You keep it in the fridge?

Now I do, yeah. In my wife's old sandwich box. Tupperware thing. in the freezer compartment.

Licensed, is it?

Well no. I assume you know that would be difficult. I don't carry it, now. But I've had it since she got put away.

Why?

All her bozo redneck cousins started coming after me, as if it was my fault. It all died down after a few months, but still ...

When was this?

Five years ago? So I took the Glock and went upstairs,

Ridiculous

very quietly, not putting extra lights on or anything. Searched. Started with my bedroom, at the back. All as it should be. Bathroom same. And the children's room. Opened the front bedroom door and this bloody thing came at me, leaping off the bed, dancing, on its back legs. Snarling, slashing its claws. Enormous blasted cat.

Cat?

Maine Coon. Like a fucking leopard. My wife had one, when we first got married. I can't stand cats, as it happens. Hers disappeared soon after I moved in. Anyway this one, it's out the bedroom door and past me and down the stairs and there's a clatter and it's out the cat flap.

What then?

Looked in the front bedroom, where it'd come from. I've never touched my wife's jewellery box, it's been sitting on the dressing table since she was arrested. It was on the floor, stuff spilled out everywhere, a right mess. But I couldn't be dealing with that, I just left it.

Why was your wife in prison?

Attempted murder, of me. Manslaughter of our children. She got life, as they call it.

Your children died?

Yes. Tim and Molly. Tim was seven, Molly was five. Should have been murder for them too, under the transferred malice rules, but they went for manslaughter.

You researched this?

Of course.

What happened?

She'd made me a hot chocolate. Often did before she left for the hospital. She worked nights. Staff nurse, on ITU. I must have once said I liked hot chocolate. I didn't, at least not the way she made it. Too sweet. But the kids did. After she'd gone to work, I'd tip it into their elephants and they'd have half each while I read them a story.

Elephants?

Little plastic mugs shaped like elephants. A blue one and a pink one. The trunk and the tail make handles. They'd had them since they were little, from her mum.

There was something in the hot chocolate?

Botox. Onabotulinum toxin A. They said she'd emptied out forty 100iu doses, enough to kill a seventy kilogram animal. Like me, for example. Or two smaller ones, like Tim and Molly. She got it from her day job, at the Haven. Cosmetic surgery place in Abindgon.

She worked nights in the hospital and days in Abingdon? At the same time?

Yeah.

[silence, 90 seconds]

Should I carry on? So I'd got rid of the cat and I thought that was excitement over for the night. I turned off the lights upstairs and put a rubbish bin to block the cat flap so it couldn't sneak back in. Then I flopped on the sofa again, with the last drop of brandy. Put some music on and got back to my book.

What music?

Mozart. Piano Concerto number twenty-one. And it was just a tiny creak, like a floorboard. Upstairs. It came at that point in the second movement, when it's gone up, tum, te tum, te tum, and it holds for a fraction of a second before it starts back down, tum-te-tum-te-tum-tum. In that little moment, it stood out so clear. Really creepy. So I went to the bottom of the stairs, on tip-toe. And just waited, looking up.

With a gun?

With the Glock, yes. It felt quite light, I remember noticing. And cold. I'd no intention of using it.

How long had it been in the freezer?

Dunno.

But you were confident it would work?

Never occurred to me that it wouldn't.

Go on. What happened?

Well it was dark up there, just a tiny bit of light from the landing window. Then this noise behind me, from the room where I'd been reading. I looked, couldn't tell what it was. Maybe twigs on the window. But when I looked back up the stairs, someone was there, standing absolutely still, in the dark. Couldn't tell who. No idea. But someone, just standing there. There was this loud bang, I thought they'd shot at me. So I shot back. I didn't know it could be her. Last thing I expected. Thought she'd be inside for another three years at least. They'd written and phoned, but I hadn't opened the letters or listened back to my voice messages, had I? Because I'd been away all week, on the station. I was very upset. I called you guys straight away. And the ambulance.

What about her? She was ...?

She was dead, yes. So when I opened my letters ...

You shot your wife and then opened your letters?

While I was waiting. And found out what had happened. The Criminal Cases Review Commission had found her conviction unsound. Because of the Botox evidence. The Botox couldn't have come from where she worked, apparently.

Ex-wife, you said. You divorced her? When she was convicted?

I did, yeah. Wouldn't you? But she must have got it from somewhere. What else do they think happened? That I got the Botox, poisoned the kids, and framed her so she'd be put away?

I'm guessing that's what her redneck cousins thought.

It is. Exactly. And you think I knew she was coming out of prison, and was sleeping on the station so when she came home, she'd find the house empty and settle herself in? Then I could come back and find an intruder, and get rid of her for good, and say it was an accident?

Funny you should say that. Almost.

Don't be ridiculous.

You had the means. You created the opportunity. What we couldn't figure out was your motivation, but I think what you've said fills in some of the gaps. And you knew about your ex-wife's release, because her Criminal Justice Social Worker came to your house twelve days ago, on Wednesday 17th July, and told you.

That's not true.

And we know you've not been sleeping on the station, because you've been in Bristol. You took a train there a week ago, and returned yesterday.

Bristol?

You went to meet a woman with whom you'd set up an internet date. Something you're in the habit of doing. You met her in a restaurant, persuaded her to take you to her home. Spent six days there, effectively holding her prisoner. You had non-consensual sex with her. You told her there was no point reporting it to the police because your father was the Chief Constable of Northamptonshire, the only thing you told her that was almost true.

Ridiculous.

PC Dodds and DS Grant transferring Mr Jarman to the duty officer now. You'll be charged later this morning. While you're waiting, I suggest you reflect on whether there are other crimes that should be taken into consideration at this time.

Recording terminated 4 a.m.

You Could Cut Hair

IT'S NOT ME, it's all them others.

Don't we all think like that, sometimes? I do, sure enough. But now and again I realise it might be me, too. It might be what I'm doing that makes relationships drift off kilter. Go sour, even. That's how I felt this morning. Naomi was doing early shift at the restaurant. Gavin wouldn't be up before midday. Bill was in HMP Bullingdon until Christmas. I had no-one to meet, nothing to do, nowhere to go. I decided to get away from Oxford and my too-familiar flat and go down to see my father. And mother of course. Always a delight.

Their place is near Amesbury in Wiltshire. All rather grand, now he's Major General Turner (Rtd). A small estate, he calls it. One village, with railway station. Two tenanted farms. Three miles of the upper Avon. It can't have been bought with family money, because there wasn't any. My dad's dad was a winder at a pit near Sheffield. I never met mother's father. She's never talked about him. My dad says he was a violent alcoholic womanising gambler who burnt a small fortune before dying of syphilis at sixty.

My dad has always kept an eye on the markets. Had the odd little punt. It's amazing how many of them pay off. He'll smile that shy smile of his, wave an unlit pipe, say 'Remember that little punt I had? Those mining stocks? Came off nicely.' And show me graphs and indices. And the next day rioters in Lesotho are being machine-gunned all over the news and I realise he's got out just in time, if you ignore violent repression and human rights and sustainability and all those bothersome issues. Insider trading, no doubt at all. Inside what, though?

He'd been in the army, then the Ministry of Defence. I never knew what he did there. Something so hush-hush I'm not sure he even knew himself. Just a cog in a wheel, he'd say. To do with Signals. He didn't do it for the salary, he did it for the *fun*, it was *interesting*. He must have made his pile from all these little punts on the side, where no-one knew as much as he did. And now he mows the lawn on his little tractor, and minds my mother, who is a perfect lush.

* * *

I could have phoned from the station for him to pick me up, but I could walk there in ten minutes. He was mowing the lawn on his little tractor when I pitched up.

'Oh, look at that,' I said. 'A peacock! Is it yours?'

'I brought seven in,' he said. 'A little punt came off. Just had a feeling. Black Rock, did I mention when you phoned? Celebrated with peacocks. And a few hens. Black Rocks of course.'

The river was early June blissful. Clouds of pale olive mayflies spinning round the willows, all the trout going berserk. He couldn't do it without staff, could he?

And where was my mother? Half past three, she'd be resting her eyes in the drawing room. She's a creature of habit. Gin, orange and a slice of lime for breakfast, her vitamins for the day. Coffee at eleven. Campari at twelve. At half past she'll sip a cool Riesling and look at food for two minutes, then to the drawing room. A small cognac. Rest her eyes. Tea at tea-time. Rev up for the evening with very dry martinis, ad lib. Three wines with dinner. Port after. Single malt before bed. Says she never sleeps but snores like a horse.

So it's fun, visiting them, an absolute blast. She's never sober, he's forever doing his squire thing around the estate or playing farmer in the garden. And every morning when I wake, I smell your perfume in my hair. I don't know where you are. Where are you?

* * *

Afternoon tea in the drawing room, with cucumber fucking sandwiches, god help us. My dad looks at the ceiling. My mother is gently whickering. 'Try not to disturb her,' he says quietly. 'Let's catch some trout for supper.'

She says, 'I'll come too,' her eyes still closed.

Dad says 'Sure, I'll get the wheelbarrow.' And he wheels it through the French windows and eases her off the sofa and in, and there she sits, legs spraddled over the wheel, singing 'There'll be bluebells over the white cliffs of Dover, tomorrow, just you wait and ... ' as we cross the lawn.

'Bluebirds,' dad says. 'Blue*BIRDS*.'

'Please love me, mother,' I say, quiet, so she can't hear me. 'Please love me.'

'Piss off dandelion,' she says. 'Don't be a fool.' A bit slurred. Good ears though.

Father hands me a rod, made up ready. 'Greenwell's Glory,' he says. 'Upstream. Over there.' And soon there's a small rippling ring and a tug and a fine fierce trout fighting for its life and losing.

I stick my thumb in its throat and twist its head back.

It gives a wriggle.

And another wriggle.

And lies still.

I close my eyes, draw in a deep breath. An angel with an

iPad asks would I mind rating my experience?

'Yes,' I say, meaning I do mind, but he takes it for assent. 'How was it for you?' he says. 'On a scale of one to ten.'

'Five.'

I breathe out, open my eyes.

The angel's gone, and Mother looks at me like I'm the one that's got the DTs. The fish wriggles again. I leap, stop it slithering back into the river. Too late to let it go now, with a broken neck.

* * *

My dad came back with apples, pitched them at us like hardball from sixty feet. Mother snored in the wheelbarrow. An apple bounced off her foot, rolled under a mulberry bush. She didn't notice. The unripe mulberries were pale green, almost white. I caught my apple on the full, scrunched it. Watched the river, thinking, why the fuck do I come here? And the sound of a Harley potato-potato-ing up the drive and it was Gavin, to the rescue.

I kissed mum on the forehead, hugged dad, grabbed my bag from the house and away. But I couldn't zip away this longing. Longing for a home, even one as mad as this. All said and done, I love the old buggers. Yes they're barking, but I feel better knowing it's not just me. So I changed my mind in the first ten miles or so and made Gavin turn round and run me back. Parents didn't comment. I slopped into my favourite armchair in the sitting room, what they call the green room.

* * *

Again I smell your perfume. Where are you, sweet?

And my phone vibrates, and it's you. 'Naomi. Come

down,' I say. 'Now. Gavin's just gone. I'm lonely. I miss you.'

'I'm on the train already,' you say.

'How did you know?'

I can hear her shrugging.

'I'll pick you up from the station,' I say. 'Trout for supper. I caught them for you.'

I take Dad's Range Rover. Naomi gets off at the far end of the platform, hair flapping over her eyes in a wind I didn't know was blowing. Hurries to where I'm waiting by the turnstiles and we're in each other's arms, tight. She needs a haircut. She sticks a package in my hand.

'Can't stop, sorry,' she says. 'But I brought this for you.'

Wrapped in brown paper, taped, addressed to my flat in Oxford, in Naomi's writing.

'What? Why?'

'Just had a call, have to go straight back. Emergency.'

And she's off, not looking back.

I watch her over the footbridge and onto the other platform, feeling like I've been kicked.

The northbound pulls in. I wait until it pulls out. She's still not looking. I head back to the house, wondering what that was all about. And what to do. Stay or go.

What am I thinking? Stay in this nuthouse, or go back to my lover. Occasional, but still. Who's in the midst of an unspecified but urgent enough to turn in her tracks emergency. A no-brainer. Go.

I pick up my bag, put her package in it.

My dad runs me back to the station.

'Andrea,' he says. 'Your friend Naomi. She's er ...'

'What?'

'She er ... bats for the other side. As they say. Doesn't she?'

'Dad. You mean she's lesbian, do you? Dyke?

You Could Cut Hair

Sapphorooni?'

'Well. Yes. I suppose I do.'

'She's bi, I think. In practice. Or you might say she's exploring her sexuality.' I buy a single to Oxford. 'Me too, actually.' Avoiding his eyes. Did I just come out? To my dad?

'Oh,' he says. 'Well. All a bit simpler in my day.'

And look where that got you, I think. You're in love with trout and she's in love with bottles. But don't say.

'How old are you now?' he says. 'Twenty-erm, isn't it? Three? Four?'

'Twenty-eight.'

'Twenty-eight. Goodness. And still exploring, are you?'

'Some of us see the whole of life as an exploration,' I say. Kiss him on the nose and go through to the platform. 'So long. And thanks ... '

'... for all the fish,' he says, with his sad shy smile, waving a sad hand.

* * *

I sleep on the train and feel wrung out when I get back to the flat. I take a cold beer from the fridge, open it, sip.

Whatever it is I want, it's not beer.

I pour it down the sink. Empty my bag on the table. I'm looking for something. What?

Book, phone, wash bag, make-up bag. Clean clothes, dirty clothes. A pack of Pontefract Cakes. Dad must have slipped them in, bless him. A pair of scissors I don't remember having. Similar to those in dad's fishing kit, that I used earlier. An article about Hayek saying he wasn't as bad as people make out. Like fuck. A dog's leash, not that I have a dog. Two dice. Three keys on a key-ring. Not mine. Whose? Cigarette lighter, ditto. Another book, a translation from the

Japanese, that I haven't read and don't recognise. NG written on the inside. Naomi's. What's that doing there? It's not as if I go round gathering up other people's possessions, is it.

And Naomi's package, from the station. That's what I was looking for. So well wrapped it's impenetrable. Scissors, I need. I had some a minute ago. Snippety snip. Must be somewhere.

Here. Under Hayek.

I hack away and get it open, and what do I find?

Scissors!

How strange. Kind, I suppose. Scissors always come in handy. But did she come all the way down to Wiltshire to give me scissors? Could it be one of those gifts that's supposed to mean something?

I go to put them in the cutlery drawer and can't say I'm not surprised. I have so many pairs of scissors!

People don't make a habit of counting their cutlery, do they? But I count eleven pairs in the drawer. Making twelve with those like my dad's, that were in my bag. Thirteen with the pair from Naomi. So I'm well stocked. It's funny, most places I go, friends, family, you can't find scissors for love nor money. Sort of thing that people are always losing. Not me, obviously.

I ring Naomi. A man picks up. So she's exploring that way tonight, is she? If that's not too uncharitable.

'Hi Gavin,' I say.

'Who?' he says, pretending not to be who he is.

'Is she there?'

'Is who there,' he says.

He does act thick sometimes.

I hear her snort in the background. Laughing at me.

Was that her emergency, Gavin at a loose end? Fuck that.

'Naomi,' I say, feeling hurt and angry. She should be

You Could Cut Hair

exploring with me. That's why I came back.

I disconnect. Pick up the scissors, the ones she sent. Turn them over in my hand. Hairdressers' scissors. Long narrow blades. Sharp points. A little curved bit sticking out the handle.

If you hold them like a hairdresser does, your third finger tucks into the sticking-out bit and they feel snug in your hand, you could cut hair with them.

Hold them the other way, like a dagger, they feel even snugger.

She lives on Howard Street. I could walk there in five minutes.

We're Not Getting Divorced

FRANK HAD A headache. David was driving aggressively, as usual, and looked grey and washed out. Frank hated putting his life in the hands of someone else, even if they were competent and sober. David was neither.

David had grey hair, grey eyes, and grey clothes. His flesh was puffy, beaded with moisture. He was Finance Director of *nanoElectra*, and Frank's boss. They were in David's company car, a Mercedes E-Class Estate, grey, that still had that new-car smell. Perfect for the autobahn, David had said. Plenty of space for four people, their luggage, and a small dog in a cage.

Frank had lost touch with his old friends long ago. David was the closest he had to a friend now, but the hierarchical aspect cast an awkward shadow. David didn't like it if Frank beat him at golf, especially since Frank couldn't hide his disdain for the game. And if David wanted to keep drinking, Frank was obliged to keep him company - like last night, in the bar on the ferry, when they had too much cognac. Hence Frank's headache.

Frank sat next to David in the front. David's wife Mary was behind David. Frank had wanted her to sit in the front, but she'd insisted on being in the back. Mary looked greyer than her husband, and thinner. She was popping little pink pills from a blister pack that she kept in a pocket of her cardigan. Frank didn't think anyone else had noticed.

Frank's wife Michelle sat behind Frank. She'd been avoiding Frank's eyes since they docked. The ferry had woken them with grotesquely cheerful Spanish guitar music on the PA. Frank had hurried to the servery for coffee and croissants, but came back empty-handed. Michelle had been monosyllabic since. She obviously thought it was Frank's fault the servery was closed. It hadn't made for the best start to the trip.

Frank hadn't liked the idea of this holiday when David suggested it, and hadn't warmed to it since. Though the two couples met socially, they'd never even week-ended together before. But Michelle had been keen, so here they were.

As soon as they left the docks, Mary's dog Billy, a Jack Russell, had started up a shrill whine from his cage in the load space. Two hours later he was still at it. Frank sympathised. He and Billy were both picking up on the vibe, he thought.

Frank sat with his back to the door, aware of truck wheels grinding away a few inches behind him. He couldn't quite believe his mental arithmetic, which said the wheels were spinning at 4,000 rpm. He sat at an angle, so he could talk with David while also engaging with the women in the back should it be appropriate. At the moment it wasn't.

He recalculated. 400 rpm sounded better.

He stared at the featureless flat countryside. First the Netherlands. Now Germany. And grunted occasional agreement with David's tetchy remarks about other drivers.

Frank was about to broach the rpm of truck wheels with David when he picked up on Mary saying something quietly to Michelle. Frank tuned in, ready to read lips and be amused.

'He was talking about toilet paper the other day,' Mary was saying. 'Wednesday. Before I went shopping.'

'David? Toilet paper?' Michelle said.

'Ordinary and recycled,' Mary said. 'He told me to stop buying recycled.'

Frank knew of David's impatience with anything green, especially if it came at a premium. Purchasing was within Frank's remit in Financial Accounts, and he regularly disagreed with David about company policy. Frank was still smarting from being told that it wasn't his job to protect the environment at the company's expense.

'Do you usually?' Michelle said.

'Use recycled? Yes, don't you?'

'Why?'

'The trees, of course,' Mary said. 'Vast numbers of the poor things industrially planted, monoculture grown, clear-felled, pulped, pressed and packaged, for you to ...'

'I see,' Michelle said. 'I know what he means though. Ordinary's softer, isn't it. Cheaper too.'

'Softer? Hypersensitive, are you? Or broke? But millions of trees. Every day. It's awful. I said if I'm doing the shopping, I'll make the choices. He started yelling.'

'David? Yelling?'

Michelle seemed surprised. Frank was too. Maybe yelling was something David reserved for his wife.

'He said, you might do the shopping but we both do the shitting ...'

'Oh!' Michelle squeaked. Frank covered his laugh with a cough.

'Blasted BMW drivers,' David said, oblivious to the women's talk in the back. 'That twat cut up three lanes of traffic at two hundred klicks.'

'Mmm,' Frank said. David needed sympathetic responses, but Frank was more interested in Mary's story.

'... so you'll get something we can both use, he said. I said, if you know what you're doing is wrong and you still decide to carry on doing it …'

'What did you get?' Michelle said.

'Ordinary. I decided it's not worth arguing about, in the … What does that sign say?'

'Dusseldorf-Sud 57,' Michelle said. 'Will that be kilometres?'

'Road number,' Mary said.

'A57. Isn't that our turning?' Michelle said.

'We want the A57, yes,' Mary said. 'David?'

'Yes,' David said, almost shouted.

Billy yelped.

'Shouldn't we be taking this exit?'

'Can't you make that dog be still for God's sake?' David said. 'I can't think with his whining.'

'Shush, Bill,' Mary said.

Billy whined on.

'You asked me something?' David said.

Frank's eyes followed their exchange like a tennis rally. For some reason it felt like match point. He thought David was being deliberately obtuse.

'Should we have taken that turn to Dusseldorf?' Mary said.

'Which turn?'

'The one we passed …'

'When?'

'When I asked you whether we should take it.'

'I don't know. This SatNav is useless. Bloody EU.'

David hit the floor with the accelerator and punched the SatNav screen with his knuckles.

'Let me sort that,' Frank said.

David batted him aside.

'David don't start,' Mary said.

'They use different satellites in the EU, don't they?'

Michelle said. 'Or different something. And don't you find it expensive here? Much more than it used to be.'

Where did that come from, Frank thought. We've not bought anything yet. And she's never been here before, Holland or Germany. Has she? Not with me. When we were in Spain, she was always saying how cheap things were.

'Look,' Mary said, 'here's another Dusseldorf exit.'

Frank looked. She was right. It said 57 again, on a yellow background.

'Where?'

'David, you're just driving straight past it.'

Holidays were supposed to be fun, Frank thought. This was getting less fun by the minute.

'I'm looking for junction 28,' David said. 'That's where we said we'd come off.'

'That was junction 28, for the A57.'

'Was it? Are you sure?'

'Yes.'

'Fuck,' David said, shaking his head.

Frank thought he'd try changing the mood. 'After four,' he said, hoping Michelle might join him. He counted in and sang, *'Softly a fire burns ...'*

David scowled at him, then barked a laugh, and came in with *'Shall we fall in love?'*

Surprised, Frank grinned at David, and sang, *'Softly the sea breathes ...'*

'Shall we swim?' from David.

Billy yipped.

'Why are you singing?' Mary said. 'Why aren't you turning off?'

'Let's go!' Frank and David sang together. *'Let's go!'*

They stopped singing. Frank looked back at Mary. She was staring at the back of David's head like she could turn

We're Not Getting Divorced

him to gorgonzola.

David shook his head, shrugged a shoulder.

Singing had been a mistake, Frank realised. What about telling jokes? Playing a game?

'Don't you *want* to go to Dusseldorf?' Mary said. 'It's your cousin we're supposed to be seeing.'

'To tell the truth,' David said, 'I don't.'

'So what are we doing?'

'We're stopping at the next service area. And you're getting out. And anyone else that wants to is getting out. And I'm getting a divorce.'

Wow, Frank thought. Lines like that, who needs jokes? He tried to catch Michelle's eye, but she was gazing at David.

'We're not getting divorced,' Mary said.

'Are you sure?'

'Yes.'

'How can you be sure?'

'Because ...' Mary said. For all her thinness and lack of colour, Frank thought she looked more alive than he'd ever seen her. She lifted a handbag from the floor by her feet, began to rummage.

'You never asked, did you?' she said, stopping rummaging. 'Not once.'

'Asked what?' David said.

'About my scans. Tests. I had an MRI, don't you remember? While you were away, in March.'

'Oh. Yes. What did they say?'

'Doesn't matter now,' Mary said, resuming her rummage. 'Do you remember who did the packing this morning, when we got off the ferry?'

'You did.'

'Yes. While you fetched coffee and made eyes at that cashier.'

'I didn't make eyes at anyone.'

'Yes you did. You always do.'

Mary stopped rummaging, withdrew something black and metallic.

Frank stared.

'I found this,' Mary said. 'In a case disguised as a bible. At the bottom of your overnight bag, the yellow one.' She tapped the back of David's head with the end of the barrel of a stubby pistol.

'Jesus, Mary,' Frank said, 'for Christ's sake be careful. It might be loaded.'

Michelle gasped.

Billy whimpered.

'David,' Frank said. 'She has a gun. She really does. Is it yours? Is it loaded?'

'Yes,' David said. 'And yes.'

'It's not your target pistol, is it?' Frank knew David spent time at a shooting range.

'No it isn't,' Mary said. 'His target pistol is a Smith & Wesson 22.'

'What the fuck did you bring a loaded gun for?' Frank said. They both seemed so calm, he thought, as if things like this happened all the time.

'Frankly, Frank,' David said, 'not the time to be discussing that.'

'David,' Mary said, 'we're not getting divorced. Pull over. Now. That yellow lay-by thing, coming up. Look, there.'

Frank looked. They were on a bridge, high over a big brown river.

Mary jabbed the pistol into the nape of David's neck. 'Pull.' Jab. 'Over.' Jab harder. 'Now.' Harder still. David flinched and shrank with each jab. He signalled, pulled into the refuge area and stopped, gripping the wheel tight, staring ahead.

'Get out,' Mary said. 'Everyone.'

'All right, Mary,' David said, arms still rigid. 'You've had your little joke.'

He'd be wise to be less flippant, Frank thought.

'Shut up,' Mary said. 'This is a Glock 19. Handgun of choice in the US, for self-defence, they tell me. I know who you got it from, where, how it was shipped.'

'What? How?'

'I know all about your buddies in Texas, David,' Mary said, jabbing the back of his neck again with the gun. 'Fifteen in the chamber and one in the breach. Sixteen rounds. One to the chest would be deadly at thirty feet.'

Frank thought she was serious, and that David's attitude wasn't helping. 'Mary for God's sake,' Frank said, looking her in the eye, holding out his hand, 'I'm beginning to see your problem. But this isn't the way to solve it. Give it to me, now. And we'll forget all about this … incident. And work things out like civilised people. Over a coffee. And a nice cake. Black Forest gateau. You like that.'

'Frank.' Mary returned his gaze evenly, waved the gun briefly in his direction. 'You're two feet from me. I wouldn't even have to aim. Do you get the picture?'

'I guess so.' Frank tried to breathe out slowly. He was beginning to feel really frightened. David's a fool, he thought. Mary's mad as a badger. Michelle's just staring at David like she's hypnotised.

'So get out. David, you first. Leave the keys.'

David got out, smirking like a poor poker player with an ace up his sleeve.

Mary followed, keeping the gun on David.

He's a big man, Frank thought. He moves fast on a squash court. Why doesn't he make his play? He's only a metre from her, he could rush her and get control of the gun before this goes haywire. But Mary must have sensed the possibility. She stepped back three or four paces, said 'Don't try anything.'

Frank put his feet on the ground, stood, feeling the bridge flex with passing traffic, buffeted by irregular blasts of warm air full of diesel fumes and industrial chemicals. He looked around. To the south, docks, container ships, bulk carriers. A town, presumably Dusseldorf. North, beyond the autobahn, a brown river crossed a flat plain. Cars and trucks passed, fast.

Someone's bound to stop, Frank thought. But then, why would they? Would I? No I wouldn't. He went to the back door, opened it. Michelle looked at him as if she didn't know who he was. 'We'll be safer outside,' he said, quietly. 'Just try not to upset her.' He took her elbow, helped her out.

'All of you,' Mary said. 'Up against the barrier. You too, Michelle.'

Michelle looked at David. David nodded.

What's going on? Frank thought. It's like I'm not here.

They moved slowly into position, as if they couldn't quite remember how to walk. Stood, backs to the barrier. Frank put his arm round Michelle's shoulders but David pushed himself between them. Frank was surprised, but let go of Michelle, let it happen.

'Mary don't do anything stupid,' David said.

'I won't,' Mary said. She shot him, twice, in the chest.

Frank jumped sideways.

Michelle screamed.

David fell to the ground between them.

Michelle flung herself over David, keening.

Frank's ears rang, his knees wavered. There was a smell like fireworks. He stepped around David, stood between

We're Not Getting Divorced

Michelle and Mary, trying to be a human shield.

'Frank,' Mary said. 'Put him over the rail.'

He could hardly take in her words. He looked round. Michelle was kneeling by David, clutching his shoulders, sobbing. David lay limp.

'Frank,' Mary said. 'Over the rail. Now.'

Frank knelt the other side of David, began to check vital signs. But it was obvious he was beyond help. David was around five eleven, 200 pounds. A dead weight. It would be difficult, even if he really wanted to do it.

'Frank,' Mary said. 'Now.' She fired the gun.

The bullet passed above Frank's head. Just above. He felt the breeze of its passing. He shivered. He had no choice. He hoisted David into a sitting position, then upright. Michelle stood, backed away, hands over her face, peeping through fingers. Frank levered David's body up onto the parapet. He was covered in David's blood. He looked at Mary.

She waggled the gun at him. 'Go on,' she said.

David's dead, Frank thought. It can't matter to him what happens now. Michelle reached towards him. She's trying to comfort me, Frank thought. But she was trying to reach David. Must be overwrought, Frank thought. He shrugged her off, rolled David's body over the edge.

Michelle gasped, stood on tiptoes, leaned over the parapet, moaning.

Frank didn't watch David's descent. He turned, put himself back between Michelle and the gun, kept his eyes on Mary.

'Thanks,' Mary said.

Frank glanced over his shoulder, tried to attract Michelle's attention. His wife was fixated on the puddle of blood on the ground. He turned back to Mary. 'Look, Mary,' he said, but stalled. He didn't know how to continue.

'Frank,' Mary said, 'you're the only one that doesn't know what's going on here.'

'Is that right?' he said.

'The gun was David's back-up,' Mary said. 'Plan C, in case A and B failed. He didn't know that I'm terminal, because he never asked. He didn't know he'd only have to wait a few weeks and he'd be rid of me.'

Michelle gasped, sounding more annoyed than sympathetic.

'I have weeks left, at best,' Mary said. 'Not months. Increasingly painful weeks, they say. I still have my pride though. That's why I've had an investigator following them since March.' She looked at Michelle. 'Frank, do you remember? They went away. David went on a non-existent *Investing in R&D* conference. Your wife went to a non-existent school-friend's hen party. I have every keystroke from their laptops, their phones.' Frank heard a yelp. Not the dog. Michelle. 'Plan A was to engineer a situation where you and me were caught *in flagrante*.'

I'd rather die, Frank thought.

But then, I probably will.

He turned his back on Mary, put his arms around Michelle. She was unyielding, cold, her eyes glued to the bloody ground.

'Then he'd divorce me,' Mary said, 'and Michelle would divorce you.'

'Michelle?' Frank shivered. He stood back a pace, held his wife by the shoulders, tried to make her meet his eyes. She wouldn't.

'Plan B,' Mary said, 'was to have some almighty row, with you and me on one side, him and Michelle on the other. I thought he might be starting that with his missing turnings just now.'

'Michelle?' Frank tightened his grip on her shoulders. It was like squeezing concrete. He shook her gently. 'Is this true? Have you been … seeing … David?'

Michelle head-butted Frank, hard, and rushed at Mary.

'No,' Frank shouted.

Mary shot Michelle in the chest.

Frank staggered, trying to get between them. Too late. He moved towards Michelle.

'Stop,' Mary said. 'She's dead. Listen to me.'

'Er …'

'Look after Billy,' she said. 'Put me and Michelle in the river. And the gun. Take the car. Have a holiday. Catch the boat back as booked.'

'Eh?'

'Burn all the passports and cards. Tell anyone who needs to know. Or who asks. That I'm in a hospice in Amsterdam, on an assisted dying programme, and I don't want visitors. Tell them David left me and Michelle left you and they went on to Venice together and you've heard nothing and don't expect to. Then start a new life. Or not. You could get David's job, if you want it. I wouldn't, though. You'll never get a better chance to climb out of the rut and find a path with heart in it. Good luck.'

She put the gun to her chest, smiled, winked.

Pulled the trigger.

Fell to the ground.

Frank shook his head, shocked and bemused.

He looked down at the two women. They lay side by side. Two pairs of eyes. Mary's brown, Michelle's blue. He knelt, turned Michelle towards him. Was Mary right? Was Michelle really involved with that snake David? Did he know his wife at all? Thirty years married. Now she lay still. He should be feeling more than puzzlement and emptiness, he knew. But he didn't. Maybe that came later.

There wasn't much blood. He checked for pulse, breathing. None. No response in her eyes. A bloody ooze from her upper body. His stomach heaved.

He turned to Mary. A small wound on her chest. He didn't want to see her back. No pulse, no breathing, no eye response. It sounded like she'd had nothing to lose.

He stood, took a deep breath. Looked round at the emergency refuge. The Audi with its doors wide open. The bridge. The women's bodies. Behind the Audi, cars and trucks rushed past. No-one seemed to be paying attention.

He could call the police.

He should call the police.

But wouldn't that be putting his own neck in the noose?

Yes it would. So he wouldn't.

He needed time to think about this. But not here, not now. He had a feeling there was only one thing to do, as Mary had anticipated.

He heaved her up, balanced her across the parapet. Hoisted Michelle up next to her. Eased them over, let them go together, watched them fall. Saw the splashes as they hit the water. Watched until they re-surfaced, drifting north under the bridge. At this range it was hard to tell them apart.

Something inside him broke into a million sharp pieces. But he couldn't just stand there staring. He washed his hands in the dog's bowl, emptied it over the patches of blood on the refuge area's yellow surface. Refilled the bowl, put it back in Billy's cage. Did a quick change of clothes and shoes, dropped all the bloodied stuff over the parapet, threw the gun after them.

He looked over what was left in the car. Keys on the dash. David's sports coat, wallet and passport in the pockets. Mary's bag, in the back, and Michelle's, with all their cards, passports, tickets, cash. Even a passport for Billy.

How will they identify the bodies? It won't be easy. Especially if no-one reports them missing.

He opened the cage, scratched Billy's head. Billy wagged his tail, licked Frank's hand, looked him in the eye with complete trust. Frank had always wanted a dog, but Michelle wouldn't have it. Too much dirt, she'd said. Too much fuss.

But he's a nice dog, Frank thought. He can come, wherever we're going.

He shut the doors, sat behind the wheel, adjusted the mirrors, buckled his seat belt. Started the car, pulled out. Drove east, in the slow lane, heading deeper into Germany. The morning sun warmed his face. He noticed that Billy wasn't whining.

It was David who pushed us all into coming to Germany, he thought, because of his cousin in Dusseldorf. Frank much preferred France. And it would do no harm, to be in another country.

He pulled off at the first exit, rounded a roundabout, returned to the autobahn heading west. He'd go to Brittany. There's a place called Plougasnou, near Morlaix, where you can fish for mackerel and bass off rocky headlands. He liked it there.

He started singing a song that he and Michelle wrote together, sang together, before they wed. That David had known well enough to join in with.

'Softly a fire burns, shall we fall in love? Softly you touch my hand, shall we kiss? And when our lips meet, shall we burn? Let's go ...'

Crossing the bridge, he looked across at the refuge on the eastbound side. It was empty, except for a couple of jackdaws.

He let the tears run down his cheeks, and sang on. *'Let's go!'*

A Little Pirouette
On The Landing

JOHN HUNCHED HIMSELF up on his elbow and looked at the woman beside him.

He couldn't help smiling at his thoughts, which were about love and loving and loving her. He and Beth had known each other for a long time. She was lying on her back, her chest rising and falling as she breathed in and out. She was smiling too, he wasn't sure why. Her eyes were shut.

'It's a funny old business, isn't it?' he said, knowing she was awake enough to respond.

'What business is that?' she said.

'You know. Making love. Sex. Whatever you want to call it. When I was a kid, we just said 'it'.'

Beth's eyes opened. She turned to him.

'Apropos of what?' she said. 'We're not actually doing it at the moment, are we? Unless I'm missing something.'

'No,' John said. 'Not yet. But it's a rum old do, it really is. We never do anything else that's even remotely like it, do we? Put a usually hidden bit of our body inside a usually hidden bit of someone else's body. Or vice versa. And move it about. Up and down, in and out, bump and grind. Or not.'

'It can be rather nice.'

'Quite. But when you think what you're actually doing. And what it would look like, to a third party ...'

'Some things it's best to just do, and not think about at all.'

'Yes. But everyone does it, don't they? If they can. Everyone. William and Kate. That's the Prince and ...'

'I know who William and Kate are.'

'And Donald Trump and wasn't someone saying she was Putin's cousin?'

'Fake news.'

'They were. She is. Bill and Hillary. Elon ...'

'Don't go there.'

'No. Charles and Camilla. Christ! The prime minister. I mean, everyone does it but no-one sees them. Because it's always in private. Naturally.'

'Preferably, yes,' she said. 'It's not when you're at your most dignified, that's true. And the smallest shred of dignity is all some of those guys have.'

'When I was twenty, I couldn't imagine old people doing it. Could you?'

'Like your grandparents? God no.'

'Or your parents.'

'Worse in a way. They must have at some time, else you wouldn't be there. Not when we were grown up, though. Surely.'

'How would you know?'

'True. My gran was a tubby little thing. Went to church in a hat. My grandad smelled of pipe tobacco. Had an enormous belly and a red nose. Impossible to imagine them...'

'But now, fifty years on ...'

'... we're grandparents and we still do it, yeah,' she said. 'Though we don't smoke pipes or go to church. And we're in reasonable shape, aren't we? For our age. Not skeletal, but not what you'd call obese.'

'Don't know about you,' he said, 'but for me it's better now than it ever was when I was young. If not quite so frequent.'

'As long as it's frequent enough. Is it, for you?'

'Varies, but ... It's slower. Closer. There was some celeb the other day, film star I think, did you see? Talking about how him and his equally celebrated wife don't do sex any more, they just cuddle. His words exactly. I really don't get that.'

'More generous now too. And we know what we like, and how ...'

'Yes,' he said. 'Like this?'

* * *

They lay still, her head on his shoulder. She seemed to have fallen asleep. He wasn't far off himself.

'Nice,' she said, with a slow smile, eyes closed.

'Very.'

He heard a sound. It could have been a key clumsily finding its way into a lock. 'What's that?' he said.

'Front door?'

More sounds. A key turning.

A clickety door handle.

The creak of a hinge.

'There's someone downstairs,' he said.

'Coming in,' she said. 'Must be Gary.'

'I thought he wasn't back until late this evening.'

'That's what he said. But who else has a key? Must be him.'

'What time is it? Nearly four o'clock. It's tea-time, for Christ's sake. Get up, quick.'

The front door slammed shut. The floor shook.

'That's Gary,' she said.

Someone called from the bottom of the stairs.

'Hi, I'm home. Anybody in?'

A Little Pirouette On The Landing

'Gary, hi,' Beth called back. 'Just in the shower. Down in two ticks. Put the kettle on, can you?'

'I'll put the kettle on,' Gary called up.

John pulled on some clothes, clattered downstairs and into the kitchen. Gary shrugged and smiled and loomed over him. He's so big, John thought. Beginning to get a bit of a belly, and only what? Thirty? No, thirty-two. Three. Can't be thirty-four, can he?

'Gary hi,' he said. 'What happened?'

'Hi dad,' Gary said. 'Match postponed. Waterlogged pitch. But we'd got all the way there, so we went to this pub for lunch.'

'Very nice.'

'And you know Tom?'

'Your sound engineer mate? Yeah.'

'He was there, with Emma, you remember. Who I went out with for a bit, at school?'

'I knew her mum, didn't I? From way back. Yeah.'

'Well Emma's living in Handsworth now, working in local radio.'

'Good for her.'

'Tom's moving up to join her. He's just working his three months' notice.'

'Good for him.'

'And until he does, there's a spare room in their flat. And they're saying I could stay there while I look for a job and find my own place.'

'Good,' John said.

'What?'

'Good idea.'

'Yeah. There's lots of media work, she says, they're always looking for people. So I'm moving out, I'm afraid. Heading up there tomorrow. Sorry it's such short notice. I'll miss you, but ...'

'No worries,' John said. 'It's kind of them. And we'll manage, you know? Good luck with it. Are you making tea? Thanks. I'll just tell your mum.'

John skipped upstairs with the news. But Beth had overheard. She was doing a little pirouette on the landing, grinning like a loon.

End Notes

Dear Reader,

I hope you enjoyed reading these stories as much as I enjoyed writing them.

I would love to know what you make of them. Do they hit the target of being good reading while throwing occasional light into dim corners?

Some of the characters in these stories also appear in *The Price of Dormice*, published in autumn 2024. If you've already read the novel, I hope you enjoyed catching up with old friends. If you haven't, you can get a taste of it in the following few pages, in the shape of its first chapter.

More novels and short stories are on the way, featuring some of these characters, among others. You can keep up to date with these at ***stevelunn.net***, where you can also check for author events near you, organise an author talk or reading, in person or on-line for your book group, bookshop, library or sitting room, or send me a message. Please do!

With thanks for your interest, and best wishes,

Steve

Acknowledgements

The help and support of many people have been essential to the evolution of my writing in general and these stories in particular. It's impossible to name everyone: here are some.

My writing teachers: Cathy Galvin of *The Word Factory*, and Alison Woodhouse; Elizabeth Garner, in Oxford; Elizabeth Reeder, Bea Hitchman and Mahsuda Snaith at *Moniack Mhor*; Harry Bingham and everyone at *Jericho Writers*; the excellent *Authors Publish* people in Toronto.

My mentors, editorial advisors and friends, especially Patricia Murphy, Joan Solomon, Adam Twine, Pen Rendall, Linda Proud, Alex Keegan, Geoff Tibbs, Steve Nussey, Mary Franklin, Ruth and Colin, Stephen and Ama Cooke, Morwenna Loughman, Sophie White, Colin Todd, Brian Monte of the *Amsterdam Quarterly,* the other Stephen Lunn (no relation) of Illinois and Florida, author of the excellent *Backyard Chronicles*, and Julia Silk, who woke me up to reality.

My fellow learners and workshop partners, especially Gillian Butler, Heather House, Jane Candlish, Julia Land, Miriam Moss, Ruth Leadbitter, Sabria Manseur and Siobhan Fraser, and my first, second and third readers.

The librarians who put books in our hands, put our books on their shelves, and have opened up their libraries to author events for me and my fellows.

The organisers of the *Oxford Indie Book Fairs*, my fellow members of the *Oxford Independent Authors* group, and the helpful people at *The Society of Authors* and *Writers In Oxford*.

The magnificent Marjory Marshall of *The Bookmark*,

Grantown-on-Spey, and independent bookshops everywhere. *Harcourt Open Arms*, the *Rotifers*, *Ahimsa*, the Durham lot and the Kylebhan crew.

My lovely family and friends, and most of all my wife Imogen Rigden.

Thank you all.

About the Author

STEVE LUNN WAS raised in a pit village in Derbyshire, has lived in Baden-Württemberg, County Durham, Bristol, British Columbia, West Glamorgan, and now spends a lot of time in Inverness-shire and Brittany, but lives in Oxford, where some of his short stories and his debut novel *The Price of Dormice* are set.

He has worked in education (as research fellow and lecturer at The Open University, and primary school teacher in Chadlington, Launton, Wantage, Freeland, Prince's Risborough), software (Softlink, National Express, Telecomputing, BAe, Morganite), farming (Tideswell, Lehenhof), and catering (Bognor Regis). He studied at Durham, Oxford, Oxford Brookes and The Open universities, and Shirebrook Comprehensive and Whaley Thorns schools; and co-founded Westmill, southern England's first community-owned wind farm.

Steve is a hands-on conservationist and re-wilder; an occasional guitar, banjo and ukelele player; and a maker of 2- and 3-D things that may or may not be art. His writing now focuses on short and long form fiction: in the past he has written about science, design, electronics and health education, business applications of AI, and fish. He shares home, family and a young dog with artist Imogen Rigden.

stevelunn.net
stevelunnbooks@riseup.net

Extract from The Price of Dormice

In this collection of stories, you met some people who also appear in *The Price of Dormice*, namely, Andrea and Naomi (in *You Could Cut Hair*) and two 'good cops', DS Grant and PC Dodds (in *Party Wall* and *Ridiculous*).

The Price of Dormice is a story of ordinary people rising up against over-development in Oxon – and in Bucks, Beds, Northants, Cambs, and so on.

It was first published by The Book Guild Ltd www.bookguild.co.uk

You can read the first chapter here, and if you would like to read the full book, you can scan the QR codes below or find it at any good book store.

Waterstones   Amazon UK

ISBN 978 1835740 552

Extract from The Price of Dormice

The Price of Dormice is dedicated to Catherine Robinson, who led the campaign to have some 'waste land' in Oxford designated a Town Green, and has since been a key figure in the Friends of the Trap Grounds; and to Richard Gordon, chair of the Friends of Burgess Field, a flourishing nature reserve that was a municipal rubbish dump less than fifty years ago.

To Catherine and Richard,
without whom many small beings
would never have been.

A little piece of Legoland
will set you back three hundred grand
but lizards lost and vanished vole
will halve the value of your soul.

Anonymous graffiti
found by Catherine Robinson
on the Frenchay Road Bridge
over the Oxford Canal in 1999

The Price of Dormice - CHAPTER 1

MAY DAY, A public holiday, celebrated in differing degrees and ways across the British Isles and elsewhere. Celebrated with ribbons and bells and great fervour in Oxford, where students and young townies drink all night, sing, fight and jump off bridges. Unbearable.

I live in Wolvercote on the north-western edge of the city and work in the centre. People think Oxford is all dreaming spires and scholarly dons strolling through quiet cloisters. It's not. It's always been noisy and busy, but around nine o'clock this Mayday morning I picked up a first hint that, behind the dignified facades, it's more like the Klondike Gold Rush. Not that there's any gold around.

It was a Monday. I'd come back from a morning jog and given dog Friday her breakfast. I wanted a grapefruit and went over to the shop to get one. Coming out of the shop, I saw a bus had stopped halfway round the corner, apparently waiting for three badly parked vans to move themselves. The bus was blocking the main road.

I looked both ways at the pedestrian crossing, as you do. To my right, the bus, stuck. To my left, a car coming down the hill from the railway bridge. Coming much too fast. A dark green Bentley, on the wrong side of the road. It fishtailed towards me and mounted the kerb like it was trying to run me down. If I hadn't jumped back, I'd be dead.

It purred past, the driver's window open. He stared at me, saying something unintelligible. I gave him the quizzical

Extract from The Price of Dormice

eyebrow. He was still mouthing off over his shoulder when he slammed into the back of the bus.

Ha, I thought, in the sudden silence. Then steam hissed, and children cried inside the car, and a woman's voice, quite calm, was saying, 'What are you doing? Are you mad?'

The shopkeeper looked out, decided it was none of his business, went back in. There was no-one else about. It was down to me. I ran over. Nothing to see through tinted windows. I pulled on the driver's door. 'You alright? Need any help?'

The driver pushed the door wide. 'Bastard!' he said.

'Yeah,' I said, sympathising. 'Stupid place to park a bus.'

'You bastard,' he said, hauling himself out and upright.

'Conrad, don't be ridiculous, he's only trying to help,' the woman said, still inside the car.

I backed away. The man she'd called Conrad was a balding redhead, taller than me, older. Overweight and out of shape, but not the sort to pick a fight with. I'd never seen him before.

The bus driver approached, arms spread. Conrad ignored him and advanced on me. I kept going round the back of the car and put its width between us. The woman got out. I'd never seen her before either. She was real class. Black hair, black dress, black boots. Black eye, too, which Ray-Bans and make-up didn't do much to hide. Was she one of these battered wives you read about? She was younger than the man, full of life, animated, until she looked at him and her face just emptied. I backed away from her, too.

She opened the rear door. 'Alasdair?' she said. 'Alasdair! Are you all right? Can you hear me? All of you, turn off those blasted machines! Take out the earbuds. Get out of the car! Alasdair can you hear me? Are you okay?'

'S'pose.'

'Bella? Charlotte?'

'Yes, Momma.'

'Good. Now get out, quick. It might explode.'

She turned to me, her hand out. 'Card?'

'Eh?' Was she after a bank card? Birthday card?

'Business card.'

'Oh. Yes.' I fumbled one out of my wallet.

'Give me two,' she said.

I did.

'Here's his details,' she said, passing one to Conrad. 'Mick Jarvis. He's a witness.' The other card disappeared, like magic. How did she know people called me Mick?

'A witness?' Conrad said.

'To the accident.'

'Why?'

'Don't be a buffoon. Call the police, now. And your insurance.'

'I already called the police,' the bus driver said.

Again Conrad ignored him and advanced on me. Why was he so angry? I backed up until I reached the wall by the post box. He followed, a pace behind. The road was snarling up with impatient drivers trying to turn round, so the police might be a while getting through. A small crowd had gathered around us. Someone's bound to help, I thought.

Conrad grabbed me by the shirt-front, slammed me against the wall, got right in my face. 'Stay away from my wife,' he said, half whisper, half growl.

I tried to meet his eyes and hold my ground. I should have said, I don't know your wife from Adam. I should have said, stay away from me, if you don't want your features rearranged. I should have said something, for fuck's sake. But I didn't. I'm not one for conversation before breakfast

Extract from The Price of Dormice

at the best of times, which this wasn't. All that came to mind was the Om chant, like Kanhai had us doing in Summertown Stars when we were kids, before we kicked off at football.

'Om' came out, loud and long.

'Shut the fuck up!' he said.

'Om.'

'You go near my wife again,' he said, 'I'll kill you.'

Typical hyperbole of the entitled, I thought. Probably went to Eton. 'Om.'

He hit me with a right that left me seeing stars. 'I mean it,' he said. I spat something out. Possibly part of a tooth. Tried to catch a breath. He hit me with a left that put the lights out.

* * *

I could see again. Two uniformed officers were manoeuvring Conrad into the back of a squad car and telling him he didn't have to say anything, but that anything he did say, etc.

'I'll certainly say something to the Chief Constable,' he said. 'She's a friend of mine, you know.'

'I'm sure she is, sir,' the female officer said. 'I'll be sure to mention that in my report. Will you and the children be okay, madam?' she said to the man's wife. 'I can get someone...'

'No, we're fine,' the woman said.

'And you, sir?'

I nodded. My head hurt.

'We'll be taking a statement in due course. Name, address, contact number?'

I told her.

The street returned to a weird kind of normal when they'd driven off, taking angry Conrad with them. I sat on the ground, back to the wall, exploring my head for bumps and bleedings. Three pale children stood on the pavement in front of me: a tubby red-haired boy of twelve or thirteen and two small mousy girls, twins, presumably Alasdair, Bella and Charlotte. All three looked shaken and embarrassed.

The woman knelt, put her arms round the girls. The boy backed away when she reached for him.

She looked at me, smiled, shrugged. 'Let's get you back to your flat,' she said, glancing across the street, 'and cleaned up. Can you stand? Walk?'

I rolled onto my knees, pulled on the wall to get upright, held tight for a few seconds while the world settled.

'Over there?' she said, pointing the right way. She knew I had a flat, and roughly where it was. How did she know? For a wobbly moment I wondered whether she was stalking me, then remembered she had my card, and she'd heard me give the plod my address.

I was less woozy by the time we'd climbed the steps up to my landing. I let us in, put the kettle on. Dog Friday said ya-ya-yoo to everyone, meaning hello, where's my breakfast? 'You've already had it,' I told her. The boy's eyes lit up when he saw my laptop, with its swirling mandala screensaver. 'I coded that,' I said, feeling a touch of pride. I asked if he knew Player Unknown's Battlegrounds. He shook his head. I launched it. 'Have a go,' I said. 'It's good.' I pointed the twins at some picture books that I kept for my nieces, then turned to their mum.

She pointed to a chair by the kitchen table.

I sat in front of a steaming bowl of water, milky white and fragrant with Dettol.

'Shirt off,' she said. She sponged me down, applied Savlon and Arnica.

'Are you a nurse?' I said.

She laughed. 'Just a mum. I'm Kimberly, by the way. That's

Extract from The Price of Dormice

Alasdair. The twins are Bella and Charlotte. Charlotte's the quiet one. You've hit the spot with them.'

'I didn't hit the spot with their dad. If it was their dad that decked me?'

'It was.' She sagged, suddenly small. 'I'd just told him I wanted out, as we came over the bridge.'

'Out?'

'Wanted a divorce. And he said, "Where would you go? Who'd have you? And your brats?" And I said, "There's a very nice young man in this village, actually. I see him every day. In fact, there he is." Because there you were. I'm sorry.'

'Crumbs.' I didn't know whether to feel shocked, flattered or terrified.

'I knew he wouldn't believe me if I said I'd never actually met you, so I didn't.'

I could see how her husband got the wrong end of the stick. 'You see me every day?'

'On the school run, with the kids. You're usually at the bus stop.'

'I am.' Nice to be noticed. I was between girlfriends, as usual, and she was a beautiful woman. But with three children and a homicidal husband? 'Is he really friends with the Chief Constable?'

'Don't know. He's buddies with a big shot lawyer who pulls strings for him. He'll get off.'

The doorbell rang. Her taxi, which I didn't know she'd ordered. The kids didn't want to go. I promised Alasdair I'd save his game in case he came back. I told the twins to take the book they were reading. Shirley Hughes's *Dogger*, one of my favourites.

'Before you go,' I said to Kimberly, 'can I just say...'

'Probably better not,' she said, from the door.

I raised a hand in farewell, realised there was a grapefruit in it. I wasn't desperate for a grapefruit any more. I was desperate for something, though. To get even with angry Conrad, maybe. Or to see more of his wife.

* * *

I opened my eyes. I didn't know where I was, what day it was. White ceiling, white walls, flickering strip light. Smells of cabbage, disinfectant, vomit. A grey box on my left, beeping in time with an orange flashing light. My left hand draped with canula, tapes, tubing. Beyond the beeping box, another bed and another less- than-fully-conscious man. My head hurt. I closed my eyes.

* * *

I opened my eyes again. A man sat by the bed, reading a Reacher paperback. Jaws clenched, shoulders twitching, obviously living the action. Big nose, awful moustache.

'Who are you?' I said. Or tried to. Probably sounded more like I was choking.

He looked up, put the book down, thrust a warrant card in my face. 'Detective Constable Clappison,' he said. Home counties accent with an exotic twang. 'Thames Valley Police. What's your name?'

'Mick Jarvis.'

He made a note in a beige notebook. 'Date of birth?'

'30.11.89.'

'Address?'

'3 Wytham Court, Godstow Road, Wolvercote, Oxford OX2 8NZ.'

'Next of kin?'

'Sandra Jane Cleary. My mother. Bankfoot Cottage, High Street, Finstock.' My voice was working better now, and I

Extract from The Price of Dormice

was getting irritated. 'What's going on? What time is it? In fact, what day is it? Why am I here?'

'Are you ready to answer a few questions?'

'I just did. Please answer mine.'

'Nine p.m. Tuesday 2nd May. You've no idea what happened?'

'No.'

'Your neighbour Mrs Swainston, flat 5, found you on the floor outside your flat, just after seven this evening. What's the last thing you remember?'

It was hazy; I had to work up to it. 'Tuesday. Yes. I'd been in the office all day. I had a call from your lot after lunch, asking me to make a statement about what happened in Wolvercote yesterday. Then later they said it wasn't necessary. So I came straight home. Got there around six. Collected Friday from Mrs Swainston.'

'Friday?'

'My dog. Fed her. Put something in the oven. Took her for a walk.'

I stalled. Memories were flooding back.

'You got back...?'

'Before seven,' I said. 'Something pinned on my door. A note. Not there earlier.'

'See anyone?'

'No.'

'What did the note say?'

'Don't know.'

It said LAST WARNING, but I wasn't sure I wanted to share that.

'Let me know if you remember. Did you remove it?'

'No.'

'It's likely whoever left the note removed it, after inflicting this damage on you,' he said, indicating my head, which throbbed. 'Any idea who or why?'

'No,' I said.

It could only be angry Conrad. Or someone working for him. He'd promised to kill me if I went near his wife, and I'd promptly let her lead me to my flat and tend my wounds. No point complaining to the police about him, with his friends in high places. But he was a bully. My grandad's number one rule for bullies was: never succumb to a bully's threats – it only encourages them. 'Just ignore them,' he'd say, 'or take the piss, they hate that.'

'I'm going home,' I said.

'Are you sure that's wise, sir?'

'Yes,' I said. 'Tell the nurse, could you? Hang on while they sort me out and you can give me a lift.'

Extract from The Price of Dormice

Steve hopes you enjoyed this opening chapter of
The Price of Dormice.

If you'd like to read chapters 2 to 53,
you can find *The Price of Dormice* at
any good bookshop
or on-line bookseller.

If you have any problems or need more info,
please visit
stevelunn.net
or
email Steve at stevelunnbooks@riseup.net

Thank you, and happy trails...